NAMING THE BABY

The Best of **The Claremont Review**

Selected by **Janice McCachen, Bill Stenson, Susan Stenson and Terence Young**

15/30

Foreword by **Bill Gaston**

The Claremont Review is edited by **Lucy Bashford, Erin Egan, Susan Field, Janice McCachen, Tara Orme, Susan Robinson, Mark Skanks, Bill Stenson, Susan Stenson, Terence Young**

ORCA BOOK PUBLISHERS

Library and Archives Canada Cataloguing in Publication

Naming the baby : the best of the Claremont review : stories / selected by Janice McCachen ... [et al.].

Poetry and fiction from the first fifteen years of the Claremont review. ISBN 978-1-55143-772-9

1. High school students' writings. II. Claremont review

PS8235.E2N35 2007   810.8'09283   C2007-904211-2

First published in the United States, 2007

Library of Congress Control Number: 2007931657

Summary: A collection of the best poetry and fiction from the first fifteen years of The Claremont Review, the international journal of young writers.

Orca Book Publishers gratefully acknowledges the support for its publishing programs provided by the following agencies: the Government of Canada through the Book Publishing Industry Development Program and the Canada Council for the Arts, and the Province of British Columbia through the BC Arts Council and the Book Publishing Tax Credit.

Cover design by James Kingsley
Typeset by Teresa Bubela

ORCA BOOK PUBLISHERS
PO Box 5626, STN. B
VICTORIA, BC CANADA
V8R 6S4

ORCA BOOK PUBLISHERS
PO Box 468
CUSTER, WA USA
98240-0468

www.orcabook.com
Printed and bound in Canada.
Printed on 100% PCW paper.
10 09 08 07 • 4 3 2 1

*This book is dedicated to the talented young writers
who began their journey into print
between the covers of* The Claremont Review,
*and to tomorrow's poets and storytellers
who may be inspired after reading it.*

Contents

Foreword

It's a privilege to be able to say something about this *Best of The Claremont Review*. I'm eager to do it mostly because there's a slight chance you're unaware that you are holding in your hands a unique and, I'll suggest, priceless artifact.

The Claremont Review is unique for a number of reasons. First, there are many literary journals to which we more experienced writers can submit. But *The Claremont Review* is unique as a showcase for the *apprentices* in this most difficult of trades. The earnestly brilliant but tentative poet, the shyly blossoming storyteller—they can send to *The Claremont Review*, and it is here that they are welcomed into the fold of real writers, and are celebrated, and find their first confirmation. There's simply no other place like it.

This professional-quality journal is now fifteen years and thirty issues old. It publishes apprentices from across Canada, and the United States, and also Australia, Europe and elsewhere. It's difficult to get into—for every story or poem the editors accept, far more are sent back with not only helpful advice but also the encouragement to continue. The quality of the work is that of skilled, serious writers, their individual visions as heartfelt, subtle, ironic and ablaze as more seasoned writers everywhere. One feather in *Claremont's* cap was a story plucked for the *Journey Prize Anthology*, an annual selection of the best of the literary journals, in whose company *The Claremont Review* was now included. More typically, writers first published in *Claremont* have gone on to degrees and graduate degrees in Creative Writing, have published in the established literary journals, have published books.

Priceless? Without a doubt. I won't utter another worried complaint about our post-literate culture, about the death-of-the-book, about our teenagers slumped at the omnipresent screen, about everything Orwell feared for a society no longer adept at the myriad subtleties of language. *The Claremont Review* is more than a thumb in a dam's hole—in so many ways it is the dam.

We should thank the excellent editors, writers themselves, who put together this journal year after year—not that they need thanks, since this is a labor of love. We must also thank the young writers whose work lies between these covers—but I know the best thanks will be to read what they've written and to pass their excellent words along.

BILL GASTON
VICTORIA, BC
APRIL 2007

Introduction

It was a dark and stormy night in November of 1991, when Bill Stenson first suggested that Canada lacked a decent literary periodical for young writers. He was working late in a medieval high school overlooking Georgia Strait in Western Canada, looking at a sheaf of poems his colleague Terence Young had given him. The poems were the work of a handful of young Romantics in the school's first Writing 12 class, a class Young had persuaded the school's renegade principal, John Pringle, to let him run on a trial basis for a year. Stenson couldn't contain his amazement at the quality of the writing.

"We can't simply let this work disappear," he said to his friend. "We've got to get it out there for the world to see."

Out across the strait, storm clouds gathered for another onslaught against the old school's drafty cinder-block walls. The aging oil furnace sputtered and died for the third time that day, and the rusting hot water pipes ticked and contracted as they began to cool. Young considered Stenson's words.

"What can we do?" he said finally. "We're teachers, not businessmen."

"Maybe that's a good thing," Stenson said.

In the months that followed, the pair walked into car dealerships, the headquarters of gas companies, the offices of political candidates, the private homes of wealthy entrepreneurs. They asked for money, lots of it. Sometimes they came out empty-handed, sometimes they walked away with a check for a thousand dollars. Before they knew it, it was March of 1992, and they were standing in the spacious foyer of the Oak Bay Beach Hotel in Victoria, BC, alongside writers, the head of the local university's creative writing department, government ministers, dignitaries and a few brave, young writing students who had agreed to read their poems at the launch of Canada's first international literary journal specifically designed for aspiring adolescent writers. As one person later described the event, "It was a class act." *The Claremont Review* was born.

In the years that followed, the magazine struggled with funding. A dedicated group of volunteers undertook initiatives such as "casino nights" and elaborate marketing campaigns designed to ensure its survival. Finally, after six years of such improvisation, their efforts were rewarded by the Canada Council for the Arts, which recognized both the merit of their cause and the quality of the product. During this period *The Claremont Review* also gathered a group of willing supporters like writer/teachers Susan Stenson and Janice McCachen, and dedicated fans like Mark Skanks, Susan Field, Lucy Bashford and Susan Robinson, all of whom have worked hard over the years to spread the word and keep the issues coming.

One is never certain if amazement should result from realizing how few people know about *The Claremont Review,* or how many do. Literary magazines, despite their stubborn relevance in the cultural bedrock of our country, are relatively obscure in mainstream society. Names like Margaret Atwood, Bill Gaston, Alice Munro, Leon Rooke and Michael Ondaatje sit prominently on the featured tables of bookstores as if they had been there forever. But these writers all got their start in literary periodicals. *The Claremont Review* provides this same opportunity to young adult writers from around the world. Lorna Crozier says, "Nothing means more to a beginning writer than her first publication. It gives her the impetus and courage to go on."

Good writing always has a purpose and is easy to differentiate from distant cousins residing in the sock drawers of our nation.

The existence of *The Claremont Review* has proven to be a benchmark, a training ground for those who wish to express themselves in the literary arts and find an audience that appreciates the what and how of their writing. The exhilaration that publication has proffered in individuals, families and communities around the world has been enough motivation for the cast of volunteer editors of the magazine over the last sixteen years. The outside world has also taken notice.

Kansas State University's *Literary Review Magazine* wrote: "They're good, damn it, these kids. Let us learn to read them." In 2001, Toronto's *Write Magazine* named *The Claremont Review* "Magazine of the Year" in Canada, and said, "This is the magazine to turn to if you want to see the future of Canadian Literature." An educator named Messaoudi Makram from Tunisia heard about our magazine and wrote: "i am deeply interested even though i do know sending those magazines is not free at all, i am more than sure that you will provide me with some issues which i reckon will be absolutely useful." Messaoudi was right. *The Claremont Review* has been and will continue to be a useful tool for students, educators and anyone who enjoys an insightful poem or story from time to time. Thanks to all of you for your support over the years.

Insight always surprises and its veracity is immediately recognizable. Orca Book Publishers approached *The Claremont Review* with the idea of something close to a *Best of The Claremont Review*. When this happened, we had an insight of our own—there is a literary God and he or she is watching over us. Since many of our editions are out of print, this book will provide a vital resource for literary stakeholders for years to come.

One thing that startled the editors when they tracked down the authors featured in this edition was the fact that every single one of them has gone on to lead an extraordinary life. To review the accomplishments of these writers would necessitate a separate and robust article, which will not be featured here, but whatever it takes to become a published writer obviously has a huge impact on the persona one offers the world.

Finally, we need to address the selection process itself, the difficulty it posed to the members of the editorial board, who felt torn every time they decided against including a particular poem or story. It was a bad feeling, as though they had rejected one of their own children. The reasons for exclusion were several: a balance of genres; a fair representation from the entire history of the magazine; space available in the anthology; accessibility of the authors who over the intervening years may have changed names, careers, continents. That said, we are proud of what we have chosen. These works are truly among the best we have published since 1992, and we know readers will be impressed by the talent revealed between these covers.

Information about *The Claremont Review* is readily available at:
www.TheClaremontReview.ca

Liz Ogilvie-Hindle
Visitor

I open my mouth
To let in a man
Who twists his body,
Knocking elbows, knee
Against my ribcage
And descends into
My stomach.

I can feel his
Fingers on
The surface of my
Heart, groping,
His palms wrapping around
The burning beat until
He smothers it and

Climbs out leaving
Bruised
Bone and muscle
So the next man
Will feel
Welcome.

Liz Ogilvie-Hindle
Carts of Linen

These women who've
Let men into their lives
No longer weep,
Peeling condoms
Lovers have thrown against
Walls, think nothing as they
Inhale the smoke of last
Evening's marijuana cigarette,
Careful to check for burns
Before making the beds.

Four-seventy-five an hour
And free coffee.
The dog shit on the carpet isn't as serious
As kitchenettes
Broken into,
Every pot left filthy
In the sink.

Some have been
Chambermaids
Thirty years: longer than
Any of their marriages.
They hold fast to carts
Of linen rolling down
The third floor corridor,
Looking for the staircase out.

Jessie Senecal
In the Garden

My mother crouches
Touching the dirty ground.
She is picking more tomatoes.
Already our windowsills
Are full of them
Ripening in the sun.
The garden is her second home
With walls of corn.
She is out there
digging up weeds and
Killing the slugs
That eat up her plants. I'm sure
She wishes I would live there too.

Bryn Latta
Decomposition

I pull away the plastic covering, the compost pile. Nice decomposition, I'd say. This might be the best one yet. Just the right stage too: the stalks are brown, limp, and mostly there's rich soil in there. A few eggshells. I sit down on the pile, legs dangling over the edge of the boards. I can feel the warmth on my bum. That part startled me the first time, how warm it is. I lie back, and pull the plastic back over myself. I can feel the bugs crawling underneath me, see the stars overhead. I settle back. Go to sleep, I guess, though I can never remember that.

Next thing I know, it's morning, and I go to sit up, but all I can move is my eyes, and I can only see the sky. Something is wrong, I figure. This doesn't usually happen. I hear footsteps, and somebody screams, which generally I don't appreciate after just waking up. Look, Mom, look! a kid says. There's legs on the ground! My legs always stick out from these little piles. I guess that could be startling. Then this lady's looming over me, stoops down. She picks something up. It is a human leg, which I recognize as my own. Part of one, anyways, from below the knee. Damn. She is turning toward the kid, who I can't see. Did you put meat on the compost pile again? she accuses. No, Mommy, I swear! She sighs. The plastic comes aside, making a black tent over my face. EEEEW! yells the kid. You see, when you put things in the compost, they rot, she says. And if we get rotten people in our compost all the time, we can't use it on the plants, can we? After a while, during which I listen to digging in the compost and something like the pulling of sticks, the plastic is pushed farther back. She picks me up by the ears. I am treated to a bird's-eye view of a jumble of dirty bones, out of which I recognize a rib cage with

4

some half-rotten meat dangling off it. Something is dropping out of the bottom of my head. I guess my nose is gone too, because I can't smell. The woman shakes her head, looks into my eyes, and says, The eyes are so sad, darling...

Roberta Cottam
On Wednesday Music Cleans

Because Moon is having an affair
it is always light
    i does not want to be exposed
         so...
    i draws Smile
    i suctions opaque squids onto Eyes
Eyes feel relieved
    i sprays Neck with a dying fish
pretty
    i arrives at the musical caravan on
                Wednesday

the day after i cleans
She wears a chicken scarf
a shriveled pea-gray wrap
  old
  bare
    i hides envy
                  green, green, green
cranberry tea floats up i's nostrils
Words are billowing dusty from Her rotting lungs
                (memories of a house-fire)
    i feels disgusted
Loyalty has no *friends*
    yet
    i   cannot...
Her fingertips spill freshly squeezed orange juice
into
an olive green (and white) checked bowl

the squids homed on Eyes jump free
they swim in the bowl
They drown in the   sweet juice...
        eyes are naked
they also try to jump free

But i commands them to stay...

Her palm whelps a little ochre worm
—dying fish with bulging blue marbles—
rejuvenation
 energized
the fish flies to Her palm
The worm swallows the fish and spits out the "swirly" marbles
 and
 they   break...
 on the floor

Then, with a quick flick...
Her hand plucks Smile from Face
smile squirms
 is put into ship-pottery tea-cup
She

gulps the live, slippery smile
down
Her throat.
                          smak smak

She belches and smiles…
There is a skeleton left behind on Face
Face is angry
    i says nothing

With cunning ecstasy
 and
barren gratitude
 i bids:
"Decided"

When i is gone from Her,
    i goes to a squashed puddle under the street
    i's reflection is foreign
         so…
    i uses a big black rock to draw New Smile
Face Smile
Back turns

And i knows
    next time i returns to the dust, it will be on Tuesday.

Jenny Mesquita
Men

I crave like cigarettes,
This itch in my lungs, need
To breathe the air beneath
Their knitted sweaters. Men
For awhile I ate
Like candy; before I caught
Their names their clothes
Were off.

Now I have reached
Critical mass, dangerous,
Volatile,
I knew this would happen.

In my bedroom I find corpses
On the carpet.
In the light
They cast strange shadows,
But most of all I hate the
Beating of their wings.

Bryn Latta
Pig Dreams

The moon shines on the bluff
Covered with small dry grasses,
Stubble on the back of this wild pig
Careening through the solar system,
Legs working madly at nothing,
A black-tusked boar barrel rolling beneath
A meteor-pocked rock of white
In a street full of garbage.

There is a parasite
In the pig's intestine
Chewing half-digested crab apples
From the woods, proliferating
In a colorless mass
Until the pig is suddenly
Chopped in half by a flat steel cleaver, and
Sunlight reveals the worm:
White, blind,
Feasting.

Faro Annie Sullivan
Sit Com

A forty-two-year-old man
in Medicine Hat sits on a couch beside three
remote controls
and watches *MacGyver*
with a strong sense of national pride, waiting for his wife to come
home, so together,
they can eat dinner and then later, maybe
make love.
A commercial comes on and he
turns
the channel.
In the kitchen, the tap drips into the
metal basin
and for a moment he is
distracted
but then catches an NFL replay on channel ten.

Outside, a streetlight glows along with the man's
porch light.
His wife wants to take some night classes: a sewing
class at the
YMCA or Women's Studies.
She's not sure.

He asks for more mashed potatoes not
noticing the darkness
under her eyes, her heavy serving hand. After *Cheers* he
gets up
to make some coffee. He turns on the kitchen
light

and suddenly is confused. The counters
are sparkling white
but
he doesn't know where the coffee maker is and for a
few seconds
his lips feel sore and
swollen.

Larissa Horlor
E.T.

She arrived here from Pluto
in 1984, with her mother
and one purple duffle bag,
the story she tells me each
Saturday morning at
the store in her smeared
lipstick, bright pink blush,
an out-patient pass like
a jeweled brooch on her chest.
Today she talks of a waiter
who came to her apartment last
night for some necking and a little
foreplay and how her mother thinks she is
too young for earthly intercourse,
only sixteen in Plutonian years.
She picks up the same pair of teal pants,
asking again if they will be on sale soon.
The manager tells her to move on,
shaking his head as she walks away,
antennae waving, gray hair
reaching for the sky.

Chris Eng
Chinook

Chinook—(n) a warm winter wind that blows from the
Pacific Ocean across the Rocky Mountains

Karen took her pants off
when I dared her to.
She didn't pause,
make a big deal about it,
or even blush,
and for just a minute
I think I loved her
for her courage.
She stood there
in the cold of the dug-out
shivering
goose bumps up her thighs
spoiling their paper white
smoothness
and then pulled her black cords
up again without saying a word.
She looked away
as she picked up her jacket
then leaned forward
and kissed me on the cheek
making her exit
up the worn steps
without looking back.
When I was sure she was gone
I took my jacket under my arm
and walked home

not knowing whether it was
the chill in the air
or my heart that was
making me shiver.

Kate Morton
Grandad's Plums

The tool shed is lined
with jam jars
each full of the beetles
the cousins and I collected
last July.
Outdated car parts, bicycles,
our favorite
the orange tractor
that has never worked
and the yellow canoe
unfinished for twenty years
or more,
hanging above the storm windows
threatening to fall
each time someone closes the door.

This is where
I imagine you
and Grandad
balanced on folding milking stools, the ones nobody
uses since the farm in Vulcan sold.
Each of you, fingers crossed
leaning over for a plum
hoping the rusting hinges of the stools
don't pinch.

Between you
the half-empty crate of Robinson's plums,
purple juice rolling down your chin and
Grandad with his cancerous smile
urging you to eat just a few more.

I can't count
how many times you've told the story
how many times I've imagined it
and why of all your children only I
should dread these delicate
purple bruises, the way they
blossom all over our trees.

Rylan Nowell
In a Bar

On Santa Del Rio,
I was watching God and Satan
play pool.
Satan nervous,
running a hand over his head
to hide his hairline, while
God smirked, a showoff with too much gel,
cocked his head like James Dean
or maybe the other way around.
"Hey kid!" God called,
"Y'know how t'play cutthroat?"
I ambled over—
it wasn't a long game.
The loser
had to buy a round, and
we slouched at the bar
while the waiter set us up.
Hurricane for me, something
red for Lucifer,
and The Almighty had juice,
the designated driver.

Andrea Schiiler
Animal Magnetism

In biology
we learn about
silent things
sex attractants
growing into
magnets
glue
general adhesion
our minds' eyes
swaying round
the airtight lab
brimming with muscles
heated thighs
thoughts now hostage until
the bell
when we shuffle
into halls
full and aching.

Arwen Williams
Every Woman On Her Knees

There is a dead girl in Courtenay this week;
line-ups of cars outside the school wait to drive the children away.
They found her sweater, unbloodied, near here.

Nobody I know dies naturally.
All become the news at six,
a piece of stained clothing admissible in court,
one button, loosened by force,
dropping to the cold floor of the gallery.

I don't know her.
The dead girl is faceless,
a bundle of hair ribbon, blood and wool.
But the women wield her name like a threat
while wrapping and sealing their babies.
They tie hood strings, say be careful:
"Don't stop on your way home.
If you're late it'll be your ass,
Honey."

The children march
one gumboot after another,
cameras trained on their faces.

The word in the pub is rapist today.
Thick-necked men in plaid are going home to polish their guns,
and their daughters, already knowing the frailty of their bones,
wait for the sounds of nightgowns
ripping in unison.

The grocery lines are longer in town.
Women buy meat and cans of soup,
eat at home in solemn kitchens
choking on the smells of lettuce and old dishes,
forks tight in their fists,
ready.

Maleea Acker
Mill Bay Ferry

We take the 6:00 Mill Bay ferry. Don't even realize, sitting in our car, that it's moving until we are halfway across the inlet. On the other side there are clusters of lights strung along the shore. My mom and sister try to predict which group is our landing. I study your townhouse complex and guess which one is your window.

We are coming back from Qualicum, a family of three, on Remembrance Day holiday. Lest we forget, we keep reminding each other, laughing.

I think of you and how people tell me you've picked the right time. This is a time for recalling what's past. Isn't it?

We offload. There's that same strange feeling of relief, even though technically we never left the island. Driving home, we pass dangerously close to your house. I imagine phoning you. Or even better, stopping by for dinner. After all, we are hungry.

We take the same route home I used to drive every weekend. I could do it in thirteen and a half minutes. It takes Mom seventeen.

That night I phone you, dialing every digit except the last two, a five and a four. I sit, casting my words across the bay to your room, with six months of silence between messages.

Shawn Tripp
Suzuki in the Sky

I am going down. Five balloons have popped and I am going
down. My name is Suzuki and I am a piano tuner. I live in
Japan, but my dreams are filled with America. That is where I
am going now, but I may not make it.

I sit in a crude wooden box made from my child's tree
house. To this I attached thirty-two helium balloons and lifted
off for America. I would have taken an aeroplane, but I am just
a piano tuner. Also, I am going down. Today, every two hours, a
balloon has popped. It is so like clockwork; it is scary. I am now
down to twenty-seven.

I have a cellular phone with me, but I am out of range. At
eight hundred miles off the coast no one can hear me. Not for
lack of trying though. The batteries are almost finished, and I
fear I will be able to transmit only one last plea before it is surely
dead. So I wait. I am hoping an aeroplane or boat will come by.
But at seventy kilometers per hour no boat will catch me.

I am working out what I will say. Trying to fit how they can
help into one or two sentences is difficult, but I have a lot of
time so I practice over and over, cutting corners and making
sure it is clear. I want to tell my wife I love her. Want to tell my
children why Daddy had to go away. But I don't have time. So
I write a letter. If I die, it will be in the ocean with me, and if I
live, they will not need it. It is as much for me as it is for them.
I have decided to sacrifice another balloon by setting it free with
the letter attached to it. This will give me less time but it will
mean a lot to my family.

Another balloon popped while I was writing the letter, so
when I send it, there will only be twenty-five left. The letter-
toting balloon travels up and away from me. It will arrive in
America before I do. There is nothing to do but wait.

I have a meal of cheese and crackers and coffee. I have better food, but before I die I will want a good last meal. So I save the food that was going to be my meal celebrating my arrival in America, for my death.

My ears are playing tricks on me and I think I hear a low drone in the distance. I warn myself not to get my hopes up. Then I think my eyes are playing tricks as well. But they are not; it is a plane. It is coming toward me very fast. I hope it will see me. I wave my arms to help and they change course so as not to hit me. I grab my phone and broadcast my special message, even risk mentioning the letter I sent, and wait for a reply.

It comes back worse than I could have imagined.

"I beg your pardon?"

Alia Island
Sixteen

In a borrowed '78 Civic
on a homework-free Saturday we roam
streets full of
music,
laugh at
boys falling over
themselves
making plays for
airy blonds
in short skirts.
For an instant
it doesn't matter children are starving
in Somalia
that the ozone layer is being destroyed
by the very car we are driving in.
Our only worry now
is the speed patrol
at the next intersection.

Julie Lambert
instructions

scribble on an envelope
mail me away from this
cold and damp

I am decomposing

or
sell me a ticket out
of this place, some accomplice to
the mutiny in my mind turning

thought toward sudden flight
promises of peace that come
Jesus
over and over again

Gillian Roberts
Shards on Her Shoes

At the kitchen table, she propped her head in her left hand, working through the newspaper crossword puzzle. The pen she held was filled with black ink, and there were dark smears on her fingers. It wasn't late enough yet to start dinner. Joe was standing at the sink, filling a glass with water. He drank it slowly, his back to her, one hand in his pocket.

She was thinking she'd rather not cook tonight, that maybe they could eat instead at the Italian restaurant across the road from the dry cleaner's. It had been a long time since she'd met Joe there, but she still remembered the color of the shirt he'd been wearing, the brand of his blue jeans. Back then, she'd imagined a big house in the suburbs filled with kids, expensive furniture, a cat and dog. Walking out of the restaurant after that first meeting, she'd watched as one car crashed into the side of another, spraying glass all over the road, a few shards on her new shoes.

She needed seven letters for sensitivity and came up with allergy, remembering Joe's reaction to animals, children.

Rachel Ishiguro
Creation

"Imagine being the first to say surveillance..."
—HOWARD NEMEROV

Imagine being the first to say *surveillance*. Imagine the feeling, your tongue giving birth to a new word. Feel it roll comfortably in your mouth, form it perfectly; then let it go. Your magic creator's eyes can see it shining softly, learning that it has wings. It unfurls them cautiously, tests them twice, then leaves. Soon it is everywhere, your word on other people's tongues. You try to reclaim it, but it doesn't linger in your mouth any longer, just escapes as quickly as it can, laughing. "We know each other too well. You made me," it says, and flies away. There's gratitude for you! Still, would you trade that one short moment of discovery for anything?

I mean, imagine being the first to say *computer*. Or *gravity*. Or even *paper*. Imagine how it would be to have that word to yourself for one small second and mold it. Imagine what you'd do with it. Would you whisper it softly so that no one else would hear? Would you say it with awe, or with disgust? Would you shout it? Sing it? Would you write it down in purple jiffy marker on yellow construction paper, or in leaky ball-point on the back of your hydro bill?

I know if I had been the first to say *surveillance*, I'd be proud. I'd hang it up in neon lights. I'd bake cookies in the shape of letters and serve it up to all the kids around the block. I'd say it, sing it, type it, love it, and then I'd let it go.

Jennifer Whiteford
Haunted House

I'm on the roof.

My mother is looking for me, I can hear her calling me as she waltzes around the yard, occasionally pausing to pluck a dead leaf from a plant in the garden.

"I'm up here, Mom!" I shout as I peel some dry paint off my left hand.

"Oh," she says. I can tell she's disappointed. "When are you coming down?"

"When I'm finished."

"Oh." It sounds like she's having one of her bad days. I know she wants me down there with her. "Don't get any paint in your hair."

"I won't."

My mother always worries about my hair. Right now it's tied back in two long braids. My bangs are falling into my eyes. I blow upward to keep them off my forehead. The scent of the garden drifts up on the breeze and tickles my sensitive nose. I sneeze.

I'm in my bare feet, which makes it easier to walk across the grainy shingles as I work on my paintings. I'm wearing denim overalls, faded by many washings and re-colored by unintentional paint splashes. The June sun is shining full force onto the black roof, but I don't notice the heat. Instead, I concentrate on my painting, stepping carefully around the edges of the large canvas, touching it up and frowning critically. I take periodic swigs from a bottle of water as I work, trying to ignore my mother who is making bored humming noises in the garden below. Eventually, ignoring her becomes impossible.

"I'm coming down!" I call, trying to keep the irritation from my voice.

"Oh, good," Mom replies.

I crawl to the edge of the roof and swing down, holding onto the eaves trough.

"Careful, Shelly," Mom says, her eyebrows pinched together. I jump, land on my feet and then fall to my knees on the fragrant summer lawn. I get up quickly, to show her I'm okay. She smiles.

"You look nice." She strokes one of my braids.

"Mom, I look like a slob," I say, laughing uneasily.

"I used to do your hair that way when you were younger. And those overalls...remember your little OshKosh ones?"

She's talking to herself, not to me. Maybe, at best, she's talking to my body, which serves only as a satellite, transmitting nostalgia and satisfying her out-of-this-world needs.

"C'mon, let's go inside," I say, trying to snap her out of her trance.

We walk into the house through the sliding screen door. I let her hold my hand.

My father "passed away" when I was five. "Passed away" is the term Mom uses. It always makes me angry. It sounds like she's trying to explain his disappearance to me, even though I was there when it happened. I guess she thinks I was too young to understand or to remember the incident. But I wasn't.

I remember we went to the carnival. It was somewhere way out in the country; we drove for a long time to get there. My father was singing along with a song on the radio. I realized, years later, that the song was "Brown Eyed Girl" by Van Morrison. Every time I hear it on the radio, I turn the volume all the way down.

When we arrived at the carnival I was amazed. I stared at the rides both in fear and in fascination. There was a Ferris wheel to my left, a mini roller coaster to my right and a haunted house standing ominously in front of me. The entrance to that "House of Horror" was through the mouth of a giant clown face. The clown's white face and blue eyes were faded, but the lips were as red as the roses in my mother's garden. I yanked at my father's pant leg, begging him to lift me up.

"What's the matter, Michelle, Ma Belle?" he asked. He only called me that when he knew I was scared.

Wordlessly, I pointed at the clown. He smiled.

"It's only pretend, Angel," he said. I clung to the collar of his shirt.

"Why don't we all go on the Ferris wheel?" he asked. My mother nodded her approval and my father put me back down onto the littered, muddy ground. To me, the Ferris wheel looked more frightening than the haunted house. I shivered, picturing myself falling from its grand height. I looked up at my father. He was smiling and gesturing for me to go ahead. I started slowly toward the ride, letting the sounds of the carnival surround me. My parents followed close behind. We stepped up to the platform. The man taking tickets was short and fat, with a voice that sounded as if his throat were lined with fiberglass insulation.

"Only two at a time," he said. "One a youz can't go."

My parents looked at each other awkwardly. I was upset, almost to the point of tears. I wanted them both to go with me. I needed them, one on either side of me, in case the safety bar broke and I started tumbling to the ground.

"You take her, Mary," my father said, "I'll watch."

Mom and I sat carefully on the ripped vinyl seat, and the ticket man locked the safety bar down. I held my mother's hand. My father waved. The wheel started turning.

My father got smaller as we went higher. I didn't take my eyes off him. He smiled and waved again, then shouted something I couldn't hear. Then, we were at the top.

31

"Look, Shelly, look!" my mother said, shaking me slightly. "You can see the whole carnival from up here! Look at the lights. Aren't they pretty?"

I looked up. The multicolored lights of the carnival spread out for miles beneath us. The swirls of color and brightness made me dizzy. I looked back down to where my father had been standing. He was gone.

When Mom and I were safely back on the ground, we went to look for him. He wasn't anywhere near the Ferris wheel. We checked the other rides, then the games, then the cotton candy stands. He was nowhere. Mom had an announcement made through the crackling loudspeakers, telling him to go to the front gates to meet his family. She and I waited there until dark, holding hands and praying. Daylight broke through the clouds. The fairground was frighteningly empty. My mother began to sob.

For a long time I thought the clown had eaten him.

It's another hot June day. My best friend Josh and I are sitting on my roof. He's looking at my latest painting through his blue-rimmed glasses. His shaggy blond hair is hanging in his face. I've grabbed his Detroit Tigers baseball cap and am wearing it backward over my hair which falls loose to my waist. The wind is still and the neighborhood is silent. The air is thick with the smell of our coconut sunscreen.

"It's really good," he says, running his finger delicately over the brightly colored shapes. "I see rage."

"Not rage exactly," I tell him, "more of a...frustration. Or...impatience."

"I love it."

My mother hates my art. She says it's silly, all swirls and shapes and bright colors. Nothing recognizable. Josh says he doesn't understand how anyone could hate my paintings. I once asked Josh why he liked it so much.

"Because I love you," he'd said. "You're my best friend. Your art always seems to reflect what's inside of you. It shows your true self. If I didn't love you, I wouldn't love your art."

I don't know what I'd do without him.

"Have you shown your mother the letter from OCA yet?" he asks.

"No," I answer.

I have been desperately wanting to go to the Ontario College of Art since I first heard about it in grade nine. Now Josh and I are both about to graduate from high school. He's going to Carleton to study journalism. I've been accepted at OCA.

"Maybe if you tell her you'll still be living at home, it will go over easier," he suggests.

"I don't think it will make a difference." Little things never make a difference.

Two years after my father disappeared, a postcard arrived. I pulled it out of the mailbox one day when I got home from school. On the front was an airbrushed photo of a beach, the sky an unnatural blue, the volleyball players' bodies too perfect to be real.

Mary and Michelle,

I'm sorry for any trouble I have caused. I'm now living just south of L.A. I'll send more news when I'm settled.

Jeremy

I took the postcard and hid it in the pocket of my coat. Later that night, when Mom was asleep, I snuck downstairs and burned it in the kitchen sink. No others ever came.

Mom changed after my father left. Her mind didn't seem to work the way it used to. The first time things got really bad was when I was eight years old, right after she'd taken me to the opening of a local art gallery. She nurtured my interest in painting in those early years, buying me all the supplies I requested and wordlessly scrubbing the spills off the floor and walls when my creativity got out of hand.

The gallery was a magnificent place, full of windows and color. The people were dressed more extravagantly than any I'd ever seen. My fertile imagination was nourished by these strange surroundings. Mom held my hand and walked me around to each exhibit, answering all of my eager questions. I stared at the people as much as the art, marveling over the full red lips and dark eyes of the fancier women in the crowd.

The day after that first visit to the gallery, I secretly ventured into Mom's bathroom when she was outside gardening. Rooting through her disorganized cosmetics drawer, I found a red lipstick. With inexperienced shaking hands, I rolled it across my lips, turning my mouth into a red monstrosity twice its normal size. I tried some black mascara too. It went on like football grease, and I ended up looking like I'd been badly beaten. I wrapped myself in a flowered bedsheet and clumped downstairs in a mismatched pair of Mom's high heels.

"Look at me, Mom!" I shouted, bursting into the backyard. Triumphantly, I twirled around, displaying my new self. Mom just stared.

"I'm gonna be an artist when I grow up!" I announced, twirling again. "Just like the ladies at the party!"

As soon as I said this, Mom leapt up from where she'd been kneeling by the rose bushes and ran toward me. For a moment I stood frozen in fear. I thought she was coming to spank me for getting into her things. Instead she ran past me into the house. I followed, not knowing what was going on.

Mom lay on the family room couch, sobbing violently. I asked her what was the matter. She didn't say anything, she just kept crying. I felt helpless and bewildered. I pleaded and started weeping myself, but she didn't even look up. I cried so hard my head hurt and the room started to spin. What seemed like hours went by, and Mom still wouldn't stop.

I ran up the creaking staircase to the bathroom and scrubbed my face until it was pink. Then I lay on the bathroom floor, exhausted. With my head on the fluffy pink bath mat, I fell into a deep troubled sleep.

I stayed away from Mom for the next few days. I hid in my room all day and then went to Josh's place in the evening. Mom slowly came back to the way she'd been before. She never explained the incident. I didn't care, I just wanted to forget it. I wanted things to be normal again.

Things stayed calm for a while, but later, Mom's fits of hysteria became disturbingly frequent. It happened when I announced that I was going to marry Jimmy Robinson, a boy in my third grade class. It happened when I asked for a pair of high heels for Christmas. It happened when I graduated from public school. And it happened when I got a scholarship to arts camp.

Through the years I learned to keep things from her. I knew what to say and what not to say to ensure a peaceful atmosphere around the house. But then the letter from OCA came. Suddenly everything was right back where it started. I felt like that little girl in bad makeup and a bedsheet all over again.

It's the night of my high school graduation. I've decided to tell my mother about the OCA letter. I'm not going to let guilt spoil my evening. I'm going to tell her everything and make her accept reality. I'm going to take control of my life.

Nervously, I dress and venture downstairs. I walk into the kitchen where Mom is standing in her gardening clothes.

"Honey," she says. "You're all dressed up."

"It's my graduation, Mom." I'm not sure if she can hear me.

"Oh, yes, I brought you something." She smiles.

I'm amazed. A graduation gift? It's the last thing I would have expected.

She holds up a plain white plastic bag. The grin on her face resembles the expression worn by actors on children's television shows. A kind of desperate patronization.

"Look," she says, pulling something out of the bag. "Bubbles! Your favorite kind."

She holds the tubular container of children's bubble-blowing liquid. I know the brightly colored container well. When I was younger I used to dance through the backyard blowing bubbles for hours. Now I'm about to graduate from high school.

The doorbell rings. Mom looks confused. "Who could that be, Shelly?" she asks.

It's Josh, I answer in my head, coming to take me to my graduation ceremony.

"Nobody, Mom," I say. "Come on. Let's go outside and blow bubbles."

"Really?" her face glows. "You really like them?"

"I love them, Mom." The doorbell rings again. "Let's go."

On the night of my high school graduation, while my peers are stepping forward into the future, I sit in my backyard with my mother. I stare into the velvet summer sky, blowing magic, rainbow bubbles. I watch them float away.

Carolina de Ryk
You Never Called

Nine days until Christmas, and I should be excited by now but I'm not. I'm too busy thinking and I'm thinking about you. You never called last night and though we just started going out, I'm worried. Worried that I shouldn't have gotten you that Christmas present, the one hidden in my closet, dressed in shiny red paper hiding the teddy bear inside, and I knew when I bought it that it was not your style and that it went way over my budget but I couldn't resist and now I regret it. My stomach shrinks when I imagine you, pushing your long black hair out of your eyes to see this bear, and you'll wonder what kind of girl you got yourself involved with.

It's nine days until Christmas, and I still can't bring myself to listen to Christmas music. I turn down Boney M. singing "Feliz Navidad" until it is just a faint chorus, and even then I can't sing along without getting a horrible feeling that it is too early to be doing things like this, even though it is only nine days. You asked me to decorate your tree the other night and now I don't know, because you haven't called and I'm here waiting. I couldn't possibly decorate my own tree though, because it will remind me of you and the fact that I never got the chance to trim your tree with you because you never called, and why are you doing this to me?

I can't remember what my friends gave me before school ended because I was too busy thinking, thinking that Christmas was just around the corner, and you were on my mind and I couldn't decide whether I should get you a present because we weren't officially going out, and now I wonder if I should have, even though we are going out because it's eight o'clock and you haven't phoned for a day and a half.

It's nine days until Christmas, and I'm beginning to wonder what I should do with this bear if you don't call. I can't keep it because every time I'd look at it I'd think of you and remember the fact that you never called, and I can't give it away because it was too expensive, and the store doesn't take returns until the New Year, and I don't think I can have it around that long without chewing its ears off wondering why you never called me and why I spent all that time worrying about you anyway.

Heath Johns
Hot Chocolate

My mother and I haven't always been so close. For starters, she gets on my nerves and she's always nagging me; it seems the only time she ever talks to me is when she's telling me to put on a coat, do a chore or who not to date. Then the divorce happened. The divorce did nothing for our relationship.

Before there was constant fighting, yelling, tension in the air so tight you could pluck it and make a tone. After, came the merciless land-grabbing. It got so bad I almost moved out, even though it would've meant quitting school to pay the bills. But we made it through. My sister went to college, and I ended up with my mom, and so far we haven't come to blows, so I guess that's a good sign. Probably the most trying time we've had so far was the night three days after the divorce was official.

I was going out with this girl that my mother would have described as a serial killer or a Satan worshipper, but I, at that time, chose not to judge women by their hair color. She was in the backseat of my Corvair, more than slightly inebriated. I checked on her several times on the way from the nightclub to my house, and each time, she'd sunk deeper and deeper into the floor of my car. I considered several places to ditch her but doubted she would have appreciated any of them. I decided to take her to my place so that she could sleep off the oyster shooters she had so gleefully devoured. The trick was to make sure my mom didn't see her.

As my tires hit the gravel on the driveway, I cut the engine. This was a much practiced skill I'd learned right after I'd gotten my driver's license. I cringed slightly when the brakes squeaked. They needed oil or something, but I knew that I wouldn't do anything about them. I opened the stuffed glove compartment and searched around for the spare bottle of Scope that I kept for special occasions such as this. I got out of the car and swished some through my teeth and spit it out on the grass. I checked the backseat to see if Twist had thrown up yet, tapped the car for good luck and headed for the door.

I opened the door slowly so it wouldn't creak and stepped inside. I was just about to close it when the lights went on. Oh shit, I thought, I'm busted. Then I saw my mom and she looked as surprised as I was. She said, "You're out late."

"Uh, yeah," I replied, my mind racing for an excuse I hadn't used lately.

"Did you have fun?" she asked nervously, and I relaxed. I now had the upper hand. It was no mystery that my mom was seeing someone. Probably the same one she'd been seeing during the tattered remains of the marriage.

"Oh yeah, had a real great time," I said, in my best Beaver Cleaver imitation, trying not to slur any of the words. But my mom picked up on something because she asked me if I was still seeing that Twist girl. "No," I lied, "I broke up with her a long time ago." There was a creak in the floorboards above my head.

"So," my mom said, trying to pretend the house was settling, "would you like some hot chocolate?" I knew what she was trying to do. She knew only too well that hot chocolate made me sleepy, and I knew that caffeine kept her up. She was trying to outlast me so she could get Sam out of the house, and I had to outlast her so that I could smuggle Twist in.

"Sure."

Soon I was sitting down in the kitchen. Mom poured more mix into a pot full of milk and put it on the stove to heat up. Then she said that she'd left her hair curler on and had to go up to her room to shut it off. I knew that she was going to tell Sam to hold tight and shut up for a while, but I enjoyed seeing her squirm and I didn't say anything. When she came down her appearance was a bit better and her lipstick was smudged.

She stood in front of the stove and stirred the sleeping serum. "So how's school going?" she asked.

"Fine," I replied. Mom realized she'd put in too much hot chocolate and was now trying to scoop out the sediment at the bottom of the pot. I sat there, tugging at the kitchen tablecloth, staring at her, wondering if she was tired at all. We didn't talk until the hot chocolate was ready and she'd sat down across the table from me.

"Um...," she started.

"So, house seems to be settling," I said with my biggest grin.

From behind her mug, she replied, "Aren't you going to drink your hot chocolate?"

"No, I thought I'd let it cool down a bit," I said. Then there was a knock at the door.

"What was that?" she asked.

"Sounds like the door," I said. "I'll go check it out." I swore under my breath as I hurried to the door. As I stepped out, Twist collapsed into a smelly heap in my arms. I called out to my mom that I would be back in a second and dragged her into the backseat again. This time I locked the door.

"What was that?" my mother asked when I returned. If she didn't know about Twist, she sure picked up on the worried look on my face. I hated that smile.

"Oh nothing, just a friend who dropped by," I said.

"Well, who was it? You should've invited him in. There's plenty of hot chocolate," my mom said.

"It was just...Bob, but he...had to go," I fumbled. She wasn't merciful about it at all.

And so we sat at the table, Mother in her maroon floral bathrobe, sipping impatiently at her hot chocolate and looking around, her eyes drifting anywhere but on me. Myself, I just stared right at her as if by trying really hard I could implant a hypnotic suggestion: go to bed.

"Aren't you going to drink your cocoa?" she asked again.

41

"It's too hot, I'll just stir it till it cools down," I responded again. So we sat there silently, listening to the constant clink clink of the spoon against my ceramic mug with the words emblazoned on it: *My mom's from Sweden, why'd you ask?* I've never understood what it meant; like so many other things my mother gave me, it confused me. I was just about to say to her that I knew about everything and ask her if we could just go to bed, but when I looked up at her face so full of impatience, frustration and sadness, and she saw my face full of the same things, something clicked. We stared at each other for half a second, and then like two absurd kettles past their boiling point, we started laughing crazily. We must have laughed for five minutes straight, because by the time we stopped, I couldn't see through my tears and my throat was raw. And so we talked. Just talked. About my father, life, all the things that had ever gone right or wrong in our lives, about what that stupid mug meant. The man upstairs, the drunk in the car, we forgot. All of a sudden they just seemed like trophies to beat each other over the head with. For the first time in years, I was more than her son, and she was more than my mother.

Rachel Ishiguro
Learning My Own Language

In this room, language
is still a mystery
We need this badly
First words: dog, house, food
acknowledging basics
Here, what I am saying is still concrete
"Chair" is solid enough to sit on,
"heat" strong enough to feel

When words are important
meaning is clearer,
subtlety becomes difficult,
the air is fresher
Outside are too many
innuendoes

There are words you can't use in a poem anymore,
words you can't use anywhere
when it comes right down to it,
words that don't mean what people think

You know what I'm saying:
            rose/
                  blood/
                        fear

Somewhere, we forgot to define our terms
I say: I miss you
You say: It might rain soon

Here, everybody agrees on a meaning for safety
We talk about it
You put locks on all the doors;
I give you a hug

Here, where we are learning to say
exactly what we mean
things are less complicated

You say: I understand
I say: Love
You say: Green moss growing
            and the smell of rain

Jesse Battis
Walk Into Fire

It's raining hard and the sound of it
against the glass is strangely old, like
whispers to Adam when he was still pale
and drunk in the garden. You tell
me that love is the space between the
shoulder and the one it carries, but I
can't get the beat of it. Elusive as the last
great innocent.

You are still innocent, this I know.
In your face you are untouched
and still throwing your baton straight
up to God. Only there is thunder in the
workings of you now, there is sand-bitten
glory and power that tears in the beholder
like snow and sunfire exploding beneath
every cuticle. It is a gift to be
blackened and blessed in your presence.

There is weariness in the day.
Lamps hang like sleepy little dolls
with their faces painted up and their
eyes raped by living. They are leaning out for
what you might give them. They are envious
of your strange and ancient light.

Do not answer them, though.
Do not answer the rain and refuse to hush
your own soul of its question. You
took a long time, always, in showing me
what laughter was. Love is a slow and tired
walk into the fire.

It is what you leave in your smile.

Anna Johnston
The Smallest Things Put My Feet on the Ground

The smell of your skin after a day of
gardening in the sun, the leaf that runs across
the street in front of me as I wait for
your dusty blue Chevy to take me nowhere.
The speck of blue acrylic under your fingernail,
the slight tilt of your head
when you listen to the blues.
The dandelion seed that floats in front of our bodies
as we sit on old red swings drinking beer out of the bottle.
The strand of blond hair that falls over your eyes
when you threaten a carburetor.
The paper flowers on my desk
that smell like our sheets in mid-July
and the picture you think I cannot see
in your side of the closet, the one of your old yellow lab.
The rusting nail left in the pine
at the corner of our yard where we tried to hang a clothesline.
The cobweb we never cleaned off the corner
of the television, which waves back and forth across
our favorite Roman Polanski movies.
The feel of your breath on the back of my neck
when you hold me during thunderstorms
and the sound of your footsteps on shag carpeting
when you turn and walk away from me.

Jen Wright
Obituary

The newspaper tells me
you passed away peacefully
in hospital. It doesn't
mention the morphine
that made you whistle for
a dog who died 56 years ago.
It recounts your
military service, year of immigration,
but not your charcoal sketches
of Goethe and Oma or
the fleck of white paint
on your fingernail.
It lists the family who will
miss you, names me Jennifer
when you called me Fraulein.
This slip of paper isn't
really about you.
It can't remind me of
the taste of homegrown carrots,
the smell of yellow cedar in your
workshop, or the Sucrets tin filled
with five dollars in dimes
that you tucked behind the alarm clock.
It won't show anyone how
to split a stone or
grind deer antlers to fertilize
the seedlings on the windowsill.
So I will not let those lines be
the last words
written for you.

Sheri Ostapovich
Strawberry Jam

Today for once it's not snowing like it has been all week. And not just the fluffy white snow that brings kids outside, but the hard wet snow that stings your cheeks as the wind blows into your face. I was sitting by the window watching for that little boy that always walks by, wearing those dark clothes and the wide-brimmed hat. You know, I could set my clock by him. If only he wasn't so weak. I see him every day while I'm getting the noon tea ready and watching "All My Children" while I wait for Sheila from next door to come over for lunch. He always walks by during the second commercial, and I watch him, his head held up high while he walks in such a dignified manner, like a clergyman in all those dark clothes. If only he wasn't so weak. I met his ma a few weeks ago down at the fall fair. She was there with her jams and preserves and we got talking. "If only he wasn't so weak," she said to me when she told me about the disease he had. Some kind of tumor he'd been slowly losing the struggle with. I told her that I see him every day, that he walks past my kitchen window, and she smiles, but I can tell she doesn't want to. She gave me a jar of strawberry jam. Today he still hasn't walked by yet, and I know what has happened. Sheila is banging on the door. "If only he hadn't been so weak," I say to Sheila when she walks in. "Who?" she asks. Outside, it is beginning to snow.

Helene Cornell
Winter Solace

I watch the reflection of the dancers in the window as they stretch and gab in circles about boys or mums or whatever's not dance. I glance over at one of the dancers, Ariel, and it is hard not to notice that she is fat. But I think she is beautiful. She has a style that would give you shivers if you caught her at the right moment. She wears the traditional black bodysuit and pink tights, as well as some baggy boxer shorts that hang off her long hips. No one says a thing about the shorts. I know what she is hiding. Her pale balloon skin warps in the window. Sometimes I watch her like this, and her eyes will close when she reaches or leaps, like she's trying to sustain something inside her. She breathes it all in, and she loves to dance. This is why I watch her.

Outside is an empty parking lot. Parents drop off their bundled children for the five o'clock class, and snow is sagging from a phone wire. I imagine that beyond the vacant lot is a field, where the grass is swaying in shades of yellow, and there are no gates or doors, just miles of overlapping hills. Fantasy is what protects me from the harshness of winter. I'm able to draw a quick sketch of it by scraping the frost off the glass before it is my turn to dance.

My name is called in a thick English accent, along with the names of the little ones, and Ariel. Her name is perfect. She loves the air. That's where she's happiest because it doesn't matter that she is big, it still takes her. I call the others little ones because I am a whopping five eight. Most of them barely meet my chest, and this intimidates me. In society I am average, but here I am the youngest and the tallest and the one who dares to raise a voice to the teacher. Some classes I end up watching the lesson from behind the door. I keep it open the slightest crack so that Mrs. Marr, the teacher, won't notice. I learn more from watching than listening. I watch Ariel, in all her hugeness and grace, and the little ones' speed and perfection, their muscles like rocks lined up on sticks. I have trouble controlling my lanky arms and legs and coordinating them with music. This is what separates me from the little ones. This is why I share such a common bond with Ariel, both of us so passionate and incapable.

Mrs. Marr establishes the rows we are to stand in by pointing from her wooden chair, centered in front of all of us. The music starts and I slop my way through an exercise. Mrs. Marr crosses her legs and leans over, places her hand over her mouth and whispers to the other teacher. They are Big Sister, watching over us, studying our every move. When they pick at me I do not make excuses for my actions. Sometimes it gets too much, too personal, and I will be rude or sarcastic or whatever it takes to show them they can't change me. They chat quietly, the aging ballerinas, shifting their focus from me to Ariel. The music ends.

"Ariel, it wouldn't hurt to take off ten." How dare they. Last year they spared her the public humiliation of such comments. They would ask her to stay after class, and she would hurry outside afterward to smoke in thirty below. Today Ariel nods passively and runs her fingers along a bead necklace. Mrs. Marr clears her throat and makes eye contact with me. My lips tighten.

"You could take off five," she says and turns to criticize the other dancers on their positioning or counting. And this is the first day I start to see myself as Ariel. Everyone feels sympathy and disgust for me all at the same time. Something has to be done, but I don't know what. I feel tears of sweat crawl out of my skin and I want to spit on the stupid bitch who slams her mallet words into me like a judge. The little ones raise their eyebrows and half grin, half smirk toward me as I walk to the window and start to study my face. My breath makes my features blend into condensation—my nose is dripping into my lips, my chin is falling to my neck.

Mother drags me to Safeway after class. The fluorescent lighting nearly puts me to sleep and I just want to be alone. My stomach is aching for attention, and I pound on it with a woolen fist. I don't want to be with screaming children bouncing in shopping carts or apron boys lifting cartons of Corn Pops to the top shelf. I pile four boxes of Tuc crackers into our cart. Mother doesn't notice. Mother also doesn't notice that I haven't said a thing. She finds comfort in my silence.

I will put one box of crackers in my locker at school. My schoolbag will have one box, my dance bag another. The last box will be kept under my bed for emergencies. Mother never packs me a lunch. I am a responsible individual now, according to her, and I should be able to pack my own lunches. Sometimes she gives me two or three dollars to buy dinner at the dance studio. They have nachos and Ichiban and other such treasures. I save the money she gives me and by the end of the month I have enough to buy myself a reward. This month I will eat four boxes of crackers, no matter how hungry I get, and that is all I will eat, no exceptions. My reward will be a new leotard, the kind the little ones are wearing these days: simple spaghetti straps and a low revealing back. This is my plan.

Day one at school and already I'm feeling ill. Mrs. Duff is going on about verbs and prepositions and using commas in the right spot: *Johnny who lives in Hairy Armpits Nova Scotia likes to go fishing on Sundays* and so forth. It's snowing harder than it has all week. It's so thick it reminds me of the flakes I constructed in kindergarten out of tissue paper, using the suicide-proof scissors with the round tips. I try to follow one of the falling flakes to the ground but lose track halfway through. We are asked to write our own sentences, but all I can focus on is letting my head slide into the crease of my palm to block out the sounds around me. Girls are giggling, and I can hear Mrs. Duff asking them to write one of their sentences on the board. My drool is forming a warm playground for my sleeve. The lunch bell disrupts my comfort.

As I am leaving, Mrs. Duff asks me if I am feeling ill. She pulls out a bottle of vitamins and taps a large yellow tablet into my hand.

"It will do wonders, you know." She giggles to herself and pulls her skirt down over her lacy slip. She takes one and crunches down on it. I contemplate whether I should hold it under my tongue so I can spit it out later, as I have seen in movies, or swallow it. It is sour and tart and so bitter my cheeks collapse to meet each other. Vitamins don't make you strong or healthy. I am the only one who determines my health. I thank her and she laughs and I hear her snort as I exit. I reach into my bag to find the box of Tucs. I spit the vitamin into the trashcan. Unraveling the plastic paper I sit down on a wooden bench facing my locker. The salt-filled goodness stings my lips. I do not swallow. I let the cracker get so mushy it flows down my throat with ease. Mother gave me a whole five dollars today. Maybe I'll spend it.

At the corner store a tall girl is talking to the owner over the counter. I pull my earmuffs down and eavesdrop.

"No, I turn eighteen in two days."

"Ahh. I see. Very good. What did you say?"

"Players Light."

He hands her the pack of cigarettes, and I place a comic book on the glass table. I follow her outside. She has trouble lighting it at first. Her breath is hard to distinguish from the actual smoke she is exhaling. She reminds me of Ariel, taking long drags and shifting from side to side, blowing on her hands.

"What are you looking at?" she asks.

"I dunno. It's weird he sold to you." I make a line in the snow using my feet.

"Why, don't I look eighteen?" I laugh. She smiles. She asks me if I want a drag. She says it's only a Players Light so it won't give me cancer and all that. She can sense this is my first time, but I inhale just like her and hold in the temptation to cough and ignore the dizzying pain I've had in my stomach lately.

It is so refreshing here, leaning on the bricks outside Mac's. We talk and smoke and read my comic book. I forget I'm hungry, excited that an older girl is carrying on a conversation with me about how all the teachers at school smoke drugs.

Girls lean over themselves on the wood floor in the dressing room. I have been dancing here for ten years. Right now we are getting ready for our exams and things are high strung. We have to be here every day after school until ten. This is a good excuse for me not to do my homework. It seems as if most of the others have been here for centuries. I watch three of them fight for a slab of mirror, bearing bobby pins in their teeth. They pull back their hair and wrap it into a tight matte in the center of their heads. They have been making their buns so tight for so long it has started to pull the skin on their foreheads back into their scalp. This is why I put mine in two buns on either side of my ears. The tension is evenly distributed. I remember the reactions of the others when I first started doing it. They teased me and made stupid comments. Well at least I won't have a forehead for a face. Ariel and I go outside for a cigarette after class. She says we have to hurry to finish before her dad comes. My mother always comes at her leisure. Once, Mrs. Marr noticed me as she was locking the door at ten thirty. She asked me if I needed a ride home, but Mother pulled in just as I was answering. There is one car for five family members, I tried to explain to her. She nodded with her head tilted. Stupid Marr. On most occasions, Mother arrives before ten thirty.

Ariel and I never talk. There is nothing to say. Yes, Mrs. Marr is a bitch and Yes, it hurts your feet when you get a new pair of pointe shoes. We blow thick clouds in controlled streams until we reach the yellow line on the cigarette. It is getting harder to ignore my stomach's ignorant cries. Maybe Ariel familiarizes herself with this feeling. She grinds the butt into the snow, and Mother's green station wagon drives in. I am nervous even though I know she hasn't seen me. I know she won't be able to smell it on me because she smokes and has lost all her senses. She has no ability to emote. I forget even what her laugh sounds like. I should try to get her to laugh. I buckle my seat belt and start to tell her about the crazy sentences Mrs. Duff uses for examples. Sometimes they're about wet noodles or silly people with names like Balding Bob or Satanic Susan, I explain. Mother grins and asks me how ballet went. She is always calm and alert in the car. The road seems to soothe her and she takes consolation in my decision to stare vacantly at billboards flashing by.

Whenever I feel tempted to eat I punch into my stomach as if to say "No! I'm in charge." My day is strung along until the climax: the opening of the crackers finally comes. I have gone through one box with hardly any cheating. School is blending into monotonous drills: pick up books, walk, smoke, put down books, put head down. I cannot remember specific events that happen during the course of the week. Everything else seems to lose its value when you have a goal to keep. The weather is spreading a sleepish vial on me. I am walking to class late after lunch, and the hallways are vacant and dull. The rows of yellow lockers spin past me and all of a sudden I take a deep breath. My stomach is pounding violently. The lights are spinning in foolish lines, and I extend my arm for the wall. I am pushing my stomach outside of me and nothing is coming up. My heart is like a frightened bird in a cage, and I collapse gracefully against a locker.

When I sleep, it is always a very deep and pleasant thing, and when I wake, I often feel refreshed in my surroundings. Today, when I open my eyes, I realize that I am not in my English class with

Mrs. Duff or at home with my posters. I am in a small white room with a TV much bigger than ours at home. The blankets have me tucked in too tightly and I squirm. I notice the clear tubes laced to my wrist. I remember that when you get a cut, it is best to rip the Band-Aid off quickly rather than peel it off. I rip at the white tape on my wrist. A nurse opens the door, bearing a tray.

"No, no, no, no, no!" She rushes over to me and rubs the tape down with her nail. "You need that so you can get better." Her smile is as polyester as my pillows, and I watch as she places the tray in front of me. I let my eyes roll to the back of my head and hope that when I wake this will all go away.

My mother softly chants my name into my ear. She touches my forehead with the back of her hand. She has brought me a silver tin of brownies from home and she places them on the bedside table. She does not understand. My throat feels tight and swollen and I want to tell her I'm fine, but when I open my mouth the air is too thin to use. Mother tries to ease my struggle by tilting her head toward mine, but still I can't find the ounce of effort it would take to assure her that I just need to rest for a while and then we can go home. I feel so guilty. There are so many others dying of internal bleeding or cancer or something, and here I am with my mother stroking my damp hair behind my ear as if this were my deathbed. I don't deserve this kind of treatment, I just want to go home. I just wish I were at home.

Time is hard to follow when you don't exactly have a schedule to keep. The nurse has come in and presented what seems to be a TV dinner, minus all the snazzy compartments for your peas and potatoes. I know that it's roughly six o'clock; I only wish they had put me in a room with a window so I could find out for myself. I'm assuming that these stupid tubes they have laced me up with are feeding me some kind of sedative, because I can't tell *gauche à droite* and the odd time I'm awake I feel tingly all over. It's not the same kind of tingle that a climactic piece of music would give you. It's more like I've swallowed a jar of bees. I can barely hold my head up to shovel my meal into the tin mother brought me. I doze off.

Someone flicks on the light dramatically.

"Good morning!" The doctor leafs through his clipboard and manages to balance himself on the side of my bed. He leans his face so close to mine that I'm nervous he'll kiss me. He reaches into the depths of his coat and pulls out a flashlight. He holds up my eyelids and shines the light at me. I squirm and whine. If I trusted my voice I'd tell him to stick his flashlight up his bobbing pendulous bum. Whatever look I'm giving him seems to have threatened him.

"Your mother and I have talked and we feel that you should be transferred. Your condition has stabilized now, and our best option is Sinclairs. It has a better environment for you and there are other girls there dealing with the same kind of problems. This is all part of your recovery. You need to see how important it is to treat yourself right. You do understand what I'm talking about, don't you?"

I am tired and upset and don't like the note of interrogation in his voice. I feel flushed and flooded with emotions. I focus on the bare rolling arm exposed from my nightgown. I pinch the drooping sag beneath my bicep and start to cry. Mother's face peers through the door.

"It's time for you to go." The doctor helps me on my feet and hands me a cloth which he has found in his coat. As he turns away I notice him shake his head to himself as though I have done something wrong. Mother helps me put on my coat and links my arm to hers.

The wind is bitter and sane. Today is the first day that it hasn't snowed for weeks. With every step toward the car I feel like I am popping bubble wrap with my feet. Mother and I walk arm in arm, my balance entirely dependent on hers, toward the station wagon.

Cléa Young
Tartan Skies

My Nana owns two rest homes in Northern England. The year I am seventeen she feels it is time to make a visit to the old country. She wants to be sure everything is running smoothly for all the old folks living in the homes and she needs a vacation. She is not well enough to make the trip alone, so as the oldest grandchild I am chosen to be her travel companion. We will arrive in London, then travel up to Hull, the Yorkshire city where the rest homes are located, and finally into Scotland. From the time I was born, my Scottish Nana has been painting pictures in my mind of the rolling glens, the brilliant Lochs and the tartan skies.

Belgrave Road in London is one bed-and-breakfast after another. This is exactly what Nana and I want after an uncomfortable nine hours on the plane. I think it will be easy to find a room with so many places to choose from, but I am mistaken. Nana proceeds up and down the strip, comparing prices and the number of stairs we will have to climb in each place. One of my duties as travel companion is to carry the luggage. Of course, I do not expect her to try to lift either of her fifty-ton cases, but I wonder if my body will hold out for the next three weeks. I am sitting on the bags watching the traffic in a trance when Nana finally decides on The Winchester. It is four pounds cheaper than any of the others she has evaluated.

Ach well, hen, this'll have to dae. I canee be bothered lookin any mare. I can tell she is quite pleased with the bargain.

Before we can fall asleep I have to figure out how the time change will affect when she takes her heart pills. After half an hour of checking and rechecking my calculations, I am sure. I make her a cup of tea, and at four o'clock in the afternoon we fall asleep with the September sun glaring through the open curtains.

When I wake at three in the morning I see Nana has curled her hair. She is on her bed drinking cold tea and reading her Jehovah's Witness prayer book. I watch her for a few minutes before letting her know I am awake. She looks as she has looked my entire life: a handful of black ringlets pulled up into a gold clip and her mouth painted red. When she discovers my eyes are open she begins a never-ending sentence. She tells me her legs were causing her grief last night and what she has decided to wear that day. Without stopping for breath, she asks for my help picking out a handbag from the six she's brought that will best match her skirt. Over dry toast and more tea Nana tells me how she prays for me. She begs me to open my eyes to the *Truth*. It hurts her that not one person in her family will survive Armageddon and be let through the glowing gates to the New World.

Hull reminds me of Victoria. I get the feeling it is the same size; there is a similarity to the churches, the trees and the way the air feels on my skin. On the same property as The Canadia there is a small brick cottage that Nana and I stay in for a week. The inside has not been redone since the seventies. The contrast between the orange shag rug and Edwardian-style windows is tacky and backward. Most nights we have our dinners made by the kitchen staff in the rest home. The other nights I insist on cooking because I cannot bear another plate of mashed potatoes and soggy peas. For her own good, I am supposed to be watching what Nana eats. But the one and only time I try to deny her a piece of apple pie, I feel like I am turning my best friend over to the police. I give in: tea and pie become our nightly ritual.

Some nights we are at the kitchen table talking for hours. She whispers family scandals through mouthfuls of pastry. Some of the events in her stories have occurred over thirty years ago and most of the people in them are now dead. Nana, however, imagines them outside our front door trying to hear what she is saying. Sometimes in the middle of a sentence she stops talking suddenly; these are the times I really want her to speak.

59

During the days, we take bus trips to Bridlington and York. My Nana is the queen of bargain-hunting. We search through every secondhand store we find. She buys doilies for her side tables at home, a winter coat for cousin Katie (a perfect fit), and a red V-neck sweater for me that has never been worn. Marks and Spencers is another favorite. I think she likes them not so much for their well-made wool suits but because they usually have a coffee shop on the bottom floor. There she can have a cup of tea, catch her breath and marvel over our *rare buys*.

The train ride into Scotland rolls along sea cliffs and through backyards. Nana has a napkin over her face for most of the ride because a draft that I cannot feel is blowing straight at her and she says it will make her eyes sore the next day. When she raises her eyes to look out the window, I tell her she looks like an Arabian princess.

Dinnee be daft, ye cheeky wee lass! she says, but I can see her smiling under the napkin.

When the train pulls into Greenock, I think it is the end of the line, maybe the world. The station is abandoned except for five young girls with rough accents; they are smoking and counting their change against the bright walls of graffiti. Nana has found someone to talk to. An Asian girl sits across the aisle from us.

Are ye going hame? my Nana asks her. The girl laughs. I can tell she is confused but Nana continues, *This is my hame too, forty-one years I've been in Canada, havnee lost my accent yet, have I?* Nana then breaks into song: "*On the bonnie bonnie banks of Loch Lomond.*"

Greenock is the most miserable town that we have visited yet, but I do not voice this thought. Possibly I am being too harsh; it is a dark rainy afternoon. Nana is excited to be home; she takes my arm and walks faster. She does not see the graffiti or fallen bricks. Instead she sees herself at sixteen, kicking up her heels to the bagpipes. She points to buildings and stores and tells me what was there when she was a young lass. She is my teacher and I am on a field trip. Why is it then I feel like the adult and Nana in her blue raincoat and bright lipstick is my child?

There are no bed-and-breakfasts in Greenock. Not surprising, I think to myself. After all, who would want to stay here? We take a ferry to Dunoon, a seaside town across the inlet. The ocean swells under us. It is still raining, but the sun has squeezed through. Nana and I are out on the deck. As we move away from Greenock, Nana waves and blows kisses. Greenock blows back smoke from the stacks.

My Scottish Nana and I travel the *bonnie banks* together. I am not just her travel companion, I am her oldest grand-daughter. From the time I was born she has dressed me in a kilt and taught me songs about Scotland the Brave. Finally, after waiting seventeen years, she takes me home with her. I understand why she is proud of this country. It is strong like her hands and her voice. During my three weeks among the thistles and plaid stars, I watch Margaret McAlpine's heart take root again.

Leah Rae
Naming the Baby

The day before I was born
my mother danced
at a
Joni Mitchell concert,
told everyone she met
I was a girl
because I kicked
to the tune of
"Blue Motel Room."

For 9 months
she put earphones
to her stomach,
piped in the songs of
Armatrading and
Baez,
argued with my father
to name me "Joan"
but chose
"Leah" instead.

Years later I discovered
in the baby book
at the grocery store
my name
means
weary
and yes sometimes
it is all too much
this *Hejira*,

and *Mingus*,
and I am once again a
tired fetus
humming with the
feminist voices
that argue
through me.

Erin Egan
These United Nations

In Argentina, there are women who wear white dresses like Marilyn Monroe. They drink roses steeped in honey for breakfast and tango with tourists, heavy with cowboy boots and tie-dyed wives who lace pony beads pink as hard candy through their hair. These are the days of sand and bubblegum, of children begging in the streets for a peso. Hollywood actors think they know them, go on location in France, float on barges in the river Seine and make films about the suffering of the poor in Haiti. The president commends their efforts. He flies in his personal jet to an embassy far away where there are camels and oil. People say they believe in things like justice and liberty and fast food chains, but the papers say obesity is the real killer now. And Saint Nicholas scoffs back hamburgers by the fireside. Fat, in our minds, he wears red while Japanese children sell their bodies so they might die as happy and wicked as us. Our girls crave the skin arid bones of the desert, the smoothness of a back made in Rwanda. They will follow these dieting instructions up through their tonsils; a cup of dried millet raised to quivering lips, Evian water bottled in a time where we cannot remember the definition for body or love. And still the powerful win, oil on their tongues, blood on their striped Armani jackets—good Cuban cigars and gold dust in the pockets of their worldly trousers. The wasteland of the Amazon is growing. It is crawling back into the mountains where families made of ice knit sweaters for Canadians with their teeth, Ecuadorian clothing packaged tightly in orange box crates. We believe we want this life, the freedom to die in higher elevations, to watch our breath cloud on glass windows. Anywhere but here. Silver minnows swim through canals all the way from Europe, something exotic tucked away in a remote corner of a tinker's shop. We are hypnotized with the thickness of dust, drowning in the scent of marijuana leaves mixed with cinnamon incense, shipped in tiny cigarette packets from China. We thought we knew the trade routes, these united nations—the way a forest glistens after a night of rain.

Colin Chapin
My Grad Year

I'll sit at your table
But I won't laugh at your jokes.
I'm only here for a place to eat,
A vague acquaintance.
I don't even belong to your world.
You disgust me.
But I'm finished anyway.
I'll be off to pace the hallways once more
Where I will have to steel myself for the lounge,
That miasma of backward caps and baggy jeans,
The scent of cigarettes and perfume,
Where everyone talks of drugs, of fights,
Of "rap" music or "metal"
Or whatever the hell it is you people listen to.
I'm used to the snide comments.
My habit of pacing always incites derision.
Sure I don't have two hundred friends like you,
(God knows at this rate I'll never know what a date is like)
Sure I've had twelve years
Of clumsy attempts at meeting people.
I've got the wit of a gas chamber
And the conversational skills of Harpo Marx,
And sometimes I wish one of you cowards,
You barbarous cretins
Would make good on one of your threats to "kick my ass"
That stupid phrase I've heard too often.

After the lounge I will think of after school,
Where to go for today's walk.
That cliff I've visited so often,
Jutting out of Observatory Hill
Like the middle finger of a schoolboy.
I've never seen it without a shroud of mist,
A curtain of promise
Where one step will lead me out of this force-fed hell.
But, no,
I was suicidal in grade eleven but not now,
Not when I've come so far,
Not in my grad year.

Sean Horlor
My Mother, Her Highness

My mother says she was a princess
in some Slavic country, shows me furs
hidden in the back of her closet,
shreds of white sable falling to the floor
like some pale European winter.

On Tuesday nights,
she sits, stares at the walls,
her hair a gray shroud
on rounded shoulders,
her cheeks like minted silver
in the moonlight.

In the dining room,
she runs her index finger along
the edge of the oak table,
leaves a solitary trail in the dust.

Tonight, there are purple half-moons
under her eyes. She scrubs
a frying pan in the kitchen sink,
water spills onto her pink slippers
and spreads across the regal floor.

Jenn Thompson
Silent

I like the way
The street is
Silent after snow,
How color
Breaks away
Sound
And throws it
Onto the lips
Of wild-haired children
White
Like angels
And laughing
As we did
Tasting snow
On our tongues
For the first time
Mouths open
And arms raised
Toward heaven

Dave Neale
Symptoms

They were driving over to his mother's house when he felt it, a lump in behind his left ear. Chris was scratching his head after a haircut to get all the cut hairs off so he could put on his hat when his fingernail tore at a marble-sized lump directly behind the lobe of his ear. Looking at his fingertip, he saw that the lump had begun to bleed.

Chris figured it must be a pimple, a very large pimple. He pinched at it with his forefinger and his thumb, like he was bursting open a grape, trying to pop the blemish. At twenty-four, he wanted to be too old to suffer from this pubescent problem.

Chris's girlfriend, Laura, sat in the passenger seat and noticed him poking and prodding at the far side of his head. She'd watch him squeeze and pick, grimacing in pain, smell and study his finger.

"What's wrong baby? Something in your ear?" Laura asked.

"No, just itchy," Chris replied, embarrassed to tell Laura that he, a grown man, had a zit. "I think it's just some cut hairs on my ear."

Chris continued to pick at the lump, periodically scratching the rest of his head so that Laura wouldn't wonder why only his ear was itchy and ask to see it.

The lump stopped bleeding but still wouldn't pop like a pimple and this had Chris worried. What could it be? He thought it could be an old welt or bruise from his hockey game on Tuesday, but Chris couldn't remember being hit. The hairdresser never nicked him with the razor either, never even mentioned a lump there.

"Hey, Laura, when your uncle had brain cancer, did he have any noticeable lumps or bumps on the outside of his head?" Chris asked as he began to fear the worst.

"I think so," she answered hesitantly, "but they only detected it when he went to the hospital with chronic headaches and dizziness. Why?"

"No reason, just wondering," Chris said defensively with a slight crack in his voice. He thought he could feel a pounding in his head and his eyes began to water. The road appeared flimsy like a Hot-Wheels racetrack.

"He also had a fever and was constantly sweating," Laura continued.

"Really?" Chris took off his jacket and thought that his sweaty forehead was warmer than usual. He really started to worry. He was rapidly feeling all the symptoms of brain cancer that normally took years to develop. Two hours ago, he'd felt fine. He hadn't had a fever, no dizziness and no headache; Chris was not even sure if he had the lump then. At this rate, he'd thought, without help or a miracle he only had an hour or two to live.

Chris began to study his lump carefully. It was firm and felt like it was attached to his head with a string or tail. It was round and seemed to be dimpled like a golf ball. Chris pulled at it, lifting it away from his head. He was certain that if he could cut it out before it spread, he would live. He and Laura did not have time to go to a hospital, so he'd have to do it himself. He knew that this self-amputation would hurt, but some people pay good money these days for piercing or scarring their bodies merely for the sake of looking good. Self-mutilation had become an acceptable activity in the nineties.

"How fast can tumors grow?"

"Why are you so interested in my uncle and his cancer all of a sudden?" Laura snapped.

"Calm down! I'm just curious, that's all."

"Well, I think it varies, but supposedly tumors grow faster in the brain than anywhere else in your body."

"Shoot!" Chris muttered.

"What?" Laura asked.

"Nothing. Do you have any scissors in your purse?" Chris was desperate.

"Sure; they're really rusty though. What do you need 'em for?" Laura asked.

Chris paused. He wasn't sure if using rusty scissors in a moving car to perform brain surgery on a part of his head that he couldn't even see when he was dizzy and had sweaty palms would be that safe. He decided it would be safer to have Laura do it.

"Hey, Laura, do you have a steady hand?"

Keeley Teuber
Mother

I played Mary in the church Christmas play
finally got to smell baby Jesus
and run up the aisle lined with candles
like so many movies I had seen
I wore a burgundy robe that covered my eyes
so hot inside it felt like Bethlehem
and I wanted the baby to cool me
with his breath

(They told me I should feel blessed to play the holy mother)

That night I put on my mom's
raspberry nail polish and stood naked
in my room when she was shaving her calves
my fingertips so red and elegant
dancing between my legs for the first time

I smelt like mom

on Saturday nights when she went out to dinner
wearing long heavy earrings
her mind on sexy boys and making love

I wanted to be her so bad

And in that moment
hair on my head
innocent nipples staring back at me in the mirror

I felt like Mary

Sharon Page
Family Photograph

We speed past hills of dust
and brush in California.
The sun slants through the open window
of the bee truck.
I am barely one,
my little pink foot rests
on the head of the gearshift.
My face is flushed,
dark hair clings damply to my forehead.

Being transported to an almond orchard,
four feet behind my head, thousands
and thousands of bees.
My dad sits beside me
one hand resting on top of the steering wheel,
denim shirt, proud smile.
He smells of bee's wax.

Car seat holds my head up,
on my face
the solemn look of sleep.
We hear the highway rushing
under the truck. Dad concentrates
on the road,
hair blowing in the wind.

Tanya Reimer
Pressed Seams and Guderman Thread

My mother thinks making
Love is like sewing a dress.
You have to start
With good fabric,
And Guderman thread.

When cutting him out you have to make sure
The grain lines are straight and
Going in the same direction.
Pin your pattern firm
Then cut.

She inspects each man
I bring home the way a seamstress
Makes sure all the stitches
Are straight
Pressed flat.
And if he doesn't quite fit
She will tug and pin
So that he fits perfectly into my curves.
I know when she likes one.
Finished with the fitting
She asks if she can try him on
Without waiting for me
To wear him out or even
Take him off.

Robin Smith
Kiss Shot

The room was filled with a thin haze of cigarette smoke. The sound of pool balls clicking against each other echoed into every corner. Blue chalk drifted through the air, lightly dusting the edges of tables, and clinging to sweaty palms. Lamps hung low above the green tabletops and gave off a dim light. I held my breath for a few seconds hoping to preserve a bit of my lungs.

I tried to recall all the times I'd been here, playing pool with my best friend Shanna and whatever guy she happened to be interested in. Occasionally I'd tag along and watch the infatuated couple all night. But I put up with it because like I said, she's my best friend, and who likes to do first dates alone? As usual, the boy of the moment brought along a friend for me, so I didn't have to be the third wheel. Sometimes I wondered why she didn't just tell the guys in advance that we came as a pair.

This Saturday night it was Shanna and Matt, and Ryan for me. I checked out Ryan from head to toe, giving a slight nod of approval at the khakis, boots and tight black shirt. Nice body too. I looked up from my inspection and caught Shanna doing the same, a familiar look in her eyes.

"Do you want to break?" I asked.

Caught off guard he blushed. "No, you go ahead." I shrugged my shoulders and racked up the colorful balls, making sure number one was at the front. I gave the white ball a hard whack, sending two solids into either corner pockets.

Ryan stood there shaking his head, a slight smile tickling his lips. I smiled and turned to Shanna who was busy playfully punching Matt and flipping her hair. "It's your turn! Get your butt over here," I called.

She looked up and said, "I think I'm gonna sit this game out. I suck at pool anyway." Funny how we'd played a million times and she never seemed to get any better. She always needed her current boy toy to show her how to play.

"Matt wants to sit this one out too," Ryan said, "so it looks like it's just you and me." I could feel my throat begin to tighten. I wasn't sure if I liked it. I mean, guys go after Shanna, not me. But, I figured, who cares? I might as well have a little fun.

"Wanna put a little wager on this game?" I asked, raising an eyebrow. Shanna once told me guys love it when you use facial gestures. I thought about it for a minute. I mean going after a guy wasn't my style. Actually, I haven't had enough experience to have a "style." Maybe that's why I leave it up to Shanna; she knows about all that kind of stuff and is always telling me about the latest advice from *Teen* magazine.

"Sure," Ryan replied, "what're you thinking?"

"I don't know, maybe the loser buys drinks?"

"Sounds good. It's still your turn," he said and winked.

I felt a surge of excitement as I lined up the next shot. I missed, on purpose. Ryan bent over to line his shot, and I couldn't help noticing how nicely his pants hugged his rear. I was impressed with the progress I was making and I glanced over at Shanna to find her watching us, a slight frown forming on her face.

We played for a while, pausing to talk and laugh between shots. I would have stayed all night if Shanna hadn't tugged on my arm, digging her nails into my skin. "Lets go!" she whispered angrily. She whined, "It's getting late and I have to work tomorrow," as she rolled her eyes in Matt's direction. I knew tonight's hottie hunting had not been a success for her. I watched Matt walk over to Ryan.

"C'mon man, let's go."

"Hold on a minute," Ryan said, "we're almost finished." He turned to me. "Looks like we'll have to take a raincheck on that bet."

"No problem, but let's finish this game," I said, looking Shanna in the eye. It was my turn. I grabbed the cue and searched for a shot. As I bent down to get a better look, he slipped his number into my back pocket. I found what I was looking for and took aim. Perfect. Kiss shot.

Matthieu Boyd
The Symphony Killers

Out of the public school system
came a whole band of addicts
high on beauty, high on
oil and the fumes of gasoline. You say,
Children love music and
I guess they do
'cept these didn't,
thought Handel was a Nazi like
Schumann was a rascist like Beethoven
was a German like the soldiers were...
Maybe they weren't children—
it's not in the birthday cake,
it's in the eyes (the age I mean):
sky-blue or bloodshot, dusty light of an old soul,
dead dream
no sex or way too much
never sing in public,
whatever.
These kids never knew symphony.
Damn good thing;
violins and cellos are just
fragility and wood
even in the hands of Menuhin—
someone would tell the jocks
and the muffins
that music breaks with a crowbar
or a fist and hell yeah they'd break the symphonies
like glass.

Out of the private school system
came the men with
the mission the girls with the good thoughts
the future Harvard grads and, Christjesus,
the orphans of love. You say,
If music be the food of love and
maybe it is
'cept these days love wants a wonder drug,
not the bread of the earth or the green eggs n' ham...
These are the kids you take to the symphony.
Once they came with chains, now
with social circles
and either way, music is tied down
dead,
not safe in the hands of the teenage-angst poet,
not safe in the mouth of the beautiful singer.

Popular culture's moving
somewhere else,
somewhere beyond the Philharmonic.

Elizabeth Jones
Anne Hathaway

Shakespeare wrote
one-hundred and fifty-four
love sonnets for his mistress.
Past eternity,
literature students
learn of this passion for a woman
who was not his wife.

I wonder how she felt.
Did she spend her evenings
on a stiff oak chair,
reading Sonnet 18
beside a candle
Shall I compare thee to a summer's day?
and realize she was Shakespeare's
winter's night?

Anne was older now
more stubborn,
only married William
because she was pregnant,
didn't like his literary ways.
Writer's block often crushed her toes.
The other woman
was thought to be a Negro prostitute
or the daughter of an Italian merchant.
Historians still search for her
identity like treasure
along the bank of the Thames.

When his lover,
dark lady,
cheated on him
with his best friend,
Hath motion, and mine eye may be deceived
he spat that she was
Blacker than hell, as dark as night,
what she had done, evil
as Medieval frescoes
of the underworld
that peel off Florentine hostels.

Dear William
really was a bastard,
preaching of betrayal
like a lisp on the Moor,
as Anne Hathaway,
compensating for his absence,
masturbates in iambic pentameter
on the second-best bed.

Nathan Hudon
Let's Just Spin

Let's just spin arms outspread into another world where
nothing has form and people will like you even before seven
AM. Let's just spin on the dirty asphalt of the lot, ignore the
used condoms and broken glass and watch the bridge rise for
the crossing of lethargic ships below it. Let's just spin on the
red rusting merry-go-round at the playground where we spun
as children and let's go and see how long it takes until we are
sucked into the great beyond past the thick bars which held us
back so many spins ago. Let's just spin outside pubs and clubs
and bingo halls dizzy with the vodka in our eyes and the sweet
smell of cigarette smoke dancing around our bodies like harem
girls who spin their naked bodies on the streets of Bangladesh.
Let's just spin in the fields and gardens and crush flowers with
our spinning feet, smother them into the cold damp mud and
then spin on them some more. Let's just spin on the ocean until
we have made a whirlpool and the bodies of dead ships will be
regurgitated onto the beaches of Florida and Hawaii and Fiji
and then we'll spin some more and suck those empty boats back
to the bottom of the sea where they will spin with fish and gold
treasures and pirates' bones. Let's just spin off the cliffs and fall
spinning through the sky like the seeds of maple trees we throw
into the air as children just to watch them come spinning back
down to us. Let's just spin. Let's just spin and spin and spin again
and then let's lie dizzy on the spinning ground and remember
what it was like to spin.

Julia Thompson
Weak Sundays

Mother and I sit at the kitchen table. I try to hide behind the Sunday morning funnies, pretend to be interested in drinking my coffee, weak, with too much cream, avoid answering her questions about the night before.

In our town, girls never walk home alone after Saturday night dances at the hall. If you can't catch a ride home, you run, and if a car of boys comes driving toward you, you know you're a goner. Even then, if they get you and pull you into their cars and do what they want, no one really cares. All that really happens is the father of the boy that screwed you over comes to your house the next day and pays you off to keep your trap shut. In our town, no one really goes to the police or makes a big deal, it's just something that happens.

Last night at the hall, the Bradson boys came. Their hair was done up, you know, in the grease that makes hair dark and shiny like. They basically all looked the same, except Davey; he was the leader of the crew. He had something different to him; maybe it was the jet-black curl that was permanently between his eyes, or the way he never rolled his jeans like all the other boys. You could tell the others were his followers, they looked up to him as if he was God. They were a mean bunch, and when they showed up, everyone went kinda silent and stared at them as they stood in the doorway. They never came in, just stood outside drinking and smoking as usual. They were just there to terrorize after the dance.

Around twelve it was over and Jane and I started for home. We only lived three blocks apart. We ran all the way through the back streets in the shadows, trying to dodge the roaming cars. At Boundary Street we split up. It was on Boundary and Plummer that I heard a loud car turning around the corner. I turned to

Jane, but she was halfway down the road to her house. I started to run again, but I could already see the headlights gaining on me, reflecting off the road. The Bradson Boys were hollering with their heads out the windows. A lump in my throat grew so large I could no longer swallow. There was nowhere to go. I panicked and froze.

Mother grabs the comics from me. "I asked, how did you get home last night?"

"I got a ride," I say and pull my floral nighty over my knees.

Caroline Mitic
The Bone Yard

The day we arrived, Uncle Herb's farm was scorched and hot.
Dry dust swept around our car in billowing clouds as we headed
up the long dirt drive. Our two-week vacation had begun at last.
I rolled down my fingerprint-patterned window and stuck my
tanned face through the open space. "Hello!" I cried with glee,
as the wind swept silky strands of dark hair into my eyes and
mouth. Splotchy black and white cows looked up lazily and
then went back to grazing the lush green grass.

The car screeched to a halt in front of a white and red-
trimmed house. Familiar barn smells filled my nose. A dog
barked. Then the kitchen door swung open, and a cascade of
delighted children ran outside to greet us. A woman with a blue
and yellow dishcloth followed at her own pace, an enormous
smile pinned sloppily to her plump, rosy face. My younger
brother and sister were already greeting the farm kids. My
mother hugged the woman, my aunt Paula, as I clambered out
of the car. "Down, Rocket!" I said as a ball of brown fur and a
huge wet tongue came barreling toward me.

This had been my mother's home when she was growing
up. She had lived here with all of her brothers and sisters. The
farm had been in the family since her parents had immigrated
to Canada and built it. When my grandparents retired, they had
sold it to their son Herb and moved closer to town. Mom said
they moved so Grandpa could be closer to the golf course.

Dinner was delicious, as it always seemed to be here, in a
warm kitchen with my closely knit family. Conversations about
cows and farm machinery floated in sociable drifts around the
adults' heads as the younger kids shared unimportant secrets.
But I thought only of the barn. I wanted to go and see it right
away. It filled me with memories of my childhood. I had spent

summer after summer here for as long as I could remember. And I wanted to see Malcolm.

After a scrumptious dessert of apple and rhubarb pie, my wish was granted. "I s'pose I might as well give the tour now, seeing as we're all done with dinner," my uncle Herb said, wiping his stubbled chin with a homemade cloth napkin. I jumped from the table, anxious to see the barn again. Anxious to see Malcolm. Although it wouldn't be much different from last year, it was a tradition for Uncle Herb to show us around.

We entered the steaming milk house, where a large steel tank collected all of the milk produced by Herb's cows. Looking up, I could see milk running in and out of the smaller glass tanks, as the farm helpers milked the cows. Malcolm was not here.

We walked through a wooden door and entered the main barn. It was cooler than the milk house and smelled of sweet hay and manure. Cows bobbed their heads up and down, as though moving to the beat of the country music that blared aimlessly from the dusty speakers. "Cows are always s'posed to produce better milk when they listen to music," my uncle said. I snickered. I stood in the center of the aisle and looked up and down the long warm barn. Thick whitewashed beams held the ceiling in place. A plump housefly buzzed in the dust-hazed window nearest me. Malcolm was nowhere in sight.

We saw the new kittens and calves, and the chickens in the hayloft. I chased an arrogant rooster all around its pen until my uncle said, "Don't do that or it won't lay fresh eggs." Only when he burst out laughing, did I remember that roosters don't lay eggs. The rooster gave me a haughty cackle and looked in the opposite direction. He'd made his point clear as well.

As we were leaving the barn, I felt a cold hand grasp my waist. I turned around to face a boy my age. His angular features and pointed shoulders twisted into a grin. "So it's my old friend Catherine," he taunted. I noticed his shabby stained farm shirt, the one he always wore.

"Let go, Malcolm," I said, giving him a look of boredom, though I was relieved that he was still around. I remembered last year, when he'd stolen a chicken from the hayloft; Uncle Herb had almost fired him. Then he'd found out that Malcolm's family hadn't eaten in three days and let the incident drop. Malcolm had told me later that his mother spent most of his paycheck on marijuana. "She finds the money, and takes it," he'd said. "There ain't nothing I can do."

I looked into his stony eyes. "Why weren't you there for dinner?" I asked. He always joined Aunt Paula for her delicious dinners whenever we came. Malcolm shrugged.

"Visiting Dad at the graveyard," he said. Then he smiled in a mischievous way that made my heart beat like a loud drum. Despite his cold appearance, he was beautiful. "Are you scared of *bones*?" he asked, squinting his deep blue eyes for effect.

Oh no, I thought. He's been in the graveyard with his dad too long. He's actually gone and dug him up. But I'd grown a whole year older since the last time I'd seen him, and this did not scare me. "Then let's go to the old bone yard and see some *real* bones!" he said. I breathed in deeply. I didn't want to see his father's bones. Besides, what was he doing digging up bones anyway?

The sun was setting but the air was still warm. Slowly we walked along the road in the direction of the cemetery. Why was I doing this? I could just imagine seeing a human skeleton on the ground. Seeing Malcolm digging it up in the middle of the night. Why did such a gorgeous guy have to be so crazy?

As we neared the cemetery, I began to regret my decision to come. I wasn't scared of seeing bones; any horror movies I'd watched had cured me of that some time ago. I just didn't want to know what he was up to. I didn't want to be the one to know what he'd done.

As I could just see the first few headstones on the crest of the hill, Malcolm cut sharply to the side and we entered the forest instead.

"Here we are," he announced. I looked around in surprise. Basking in the weakening shafts of sunlight that filtered through the canopy of trees, I could see skeletons sprawled out everywhere. Some were old and half buried, others looked clean and white. But as I looked closer, I noticed that they were not human.

"We drag the dead cows here and let them return to the soil naturally and peacefully," Malcolm said. "It's the easiest thing to do when they die." Then very quietly he added, "And that over there was my favorite horse."

I looked into Malcolm's eyes, staring sadly at the skeleton of his horse, and something changed. "Were you really visiting your dad?" I asked softly. He shrugged and looked away.

"I guess so," he said, slumping slightly. There was a moment of silence. "I never really knew him. He ran away before I was born. When Mom found out he was dead, we came to his funeral." He sighed, looked up and took a step closer to me. I could see his muscles ripple beneath his old gray farm shirt.

"Besides," he said, "I wanted to scare you. But obviously you've grown up since last year." He looked at me with new respect, and the coldness I had seen before was no longer there. I didn't laugh, or even feel proud of myself for coming along. The bone yard had a different effect on me. It was a peaceful place, filled with memories. I could feel the past and the present mingled together. And most of all I could see why Malcolm spent so much time here.

"They're like the family I never really had," he whispered. "When I talk, they listen. They may be old bones, but they listen to what I say."

I'm grown now, with children of my own. Whenever I tell someone this story, I always show them the souvenir I got from the bone yard: a large cow's tooth tied on a piece of bright yellow yarn. I don't wear it often but keep it in a safe place next to the farm shirt of Malcolm's I saved. When I visit Malcolm, I don't go to the graveyard where his body lies, but instead to the bone yard.

Phoebe Prioleau
Cleavage Queen from Provence

Last summer, the summer I turned sixteen, my mom figured I needed to do something more "productive" than watch TV and hang out with my friends at Dairy Queen, so she asked some French exchange student to come stay with us. I tried to convince her it was a stupid idea—why the hell would a French girl want to live in Richmond, Virginia, with a girl who didn't even take French in school? My mom just sighed and said she hoped the kid would teach me some manners as well as a little French. I think she expected me to come away wearing a plaid jumper, white gloves and a beret. Before I could explain that I didn't plan to curtsy to the family whenever I came down for breakfast, my mom announced that everything was settled. Angelique, a seventeen-year-old who lived somewhere in Provence, would be coming to stay with us for two weeks.

My dad and I piled in the old Volvo station wagon and drove two and a half hours to pick up the French girl at Dulles Airport. Even though the computer screen said the plane had landed, we waited behind the metal bar for hours with limousine drivers holding cardboard signs and women carrying flowers for their boyfriends. Finally someone did approach us: a six-foot security guard with a pistol and two walkie-talkies dangling from his belt. When he moved to the side to talk to my dad, I caught sight of a girl in a neon green tube-top—the French kid had arrived.

She was wearing platform silver sandals that sparkled in the light and a tight black mini-skirt slit up both sides. The kid didn't smile when she saw our *Welcome to the USA, Angelique* sign that I had dashed off in the car with big bubble letters. The security guard broke the silence by explaining there had been a problem that had tied things up: Angelique had brought in a whole duffel bag of gourmet snacks from France that she "forgot" to declare in customs. When the drug-sniffing beagle got one whiff of the croissants, *pain au chocolat*, and Brie cheese, he let out a howl and of course they had to check her bags.

Angelique gazed at the Au Bon Pain restaurant on the other side of the airport and wouldn't look us in the eye.

My dad tried to liven up the car ride back with polite conversation. He's an amateur chef on the weekends, and I guess that's why he chose to talk about food. "Angelique, it was so kind of you to bring all those treats for us to sample. It would have been such a nice gift! I just adore French cheese! Camembert is my favorite—not too good for cooking, though. I'm sorry they wouldn't let you bring it all into the country!"

"Gift?" she asked, giggling, pronouncing the word with the French "ee." Her silver tongue ring reflected the sunlight. "No it was not a gift! My parents tell me ze food in America taste like zat!" She held up a miniature bar of soap she had taken off the plane.

Angelique kept her eyes focused on the bar of soap as my dad made a couple of pretty insipid comments on French cuisine. I fished in my bag for my Walkman and started listening to Red Hot Chili Peppers.

When we got home, my mom politely scanned the kid over—all the way from the silver sandals to the dyed blond hair. "Would you like anything to eat, dear?" she finally asked her when my dad had finished lugging in Angelique's suitcases.

I took the kid upstairs to my room (which was now hers) and left her alone to unpack her stuff. My mom didn't say anything when I came downstairs, but I could tell she was upset. Angelique wasn't exactly the *Madeleine* type of girl she was expecting.

The next day, Angelique rolled out of bed at two o'clock in the afternoon. "I'm sure it's just jetlag," my mom remarked as we were finishing lunch. But the next day and the day after that, she emerged at the same time. When my dad asked her what she wanted for breakfast, I gave him a vicious kick under the table. Why didn't we give the kid a bowl of Cheerios and be done with it? But of course, Angelique had to think of the most outrageous breakfast food ever. "Pain au chocolat," she replied as if pain au chocolat grew on trees. When my dad kindly explained that pain au chocolat wasn't an option, she chose blueberry pancakes instead. Dealing with Angelique's breakfast was, of course, my responsibility. I left the little stems on the blueberries just to piss her off.

After a day and a half, we ran out of things to do. I took the French girl to the mall the first afternoon with the idea of leaving her in a store and going off to find my friends. They weren't there, though, so I read *Teen* magazine outside the dressing room as she tried on as many outfits as the salesclerk could thrust through the curtain. When she spent all her money on a sixty-five-dollar pair of the tightest black jeans I'd ever seen, I realized that movies, concerts and more shopping expeditions were out of the question—my parents weren't about to pay for both of us.

So I ignored my mom's groans and sighs and brought Angelique to my hangout spot at Dairy Queen. A few of my friends were smoking in the back, near the wooden benches and the garbage bin. Mike, Liza and Ralph sat on one bench and Ralph's six-year-old brother lay sprawled out on the pavement with a handful of GI-Joes. Mike and Ralph seemed pretty excited to see a tall French girl in tight black Levis and a blue-and-white-striped bikini top. Ralph, the only one who took French in school, walked right over and started bonjouring her. Angelique didn't say anything, she just gave him a crazy look and turned bright red. But when he leaned over to kiss her on both cheeks, she slapped him across the face as hard as she could. He staggered backward a little, regaining his balance, and then walked right back over to the bench. The kid blushed even more after that, and I didn't know what to say or do, so I told Ralph "sorry" as fast as I could and escorted her out of Dairy Queen.

I was about to start complaining to my family about Angelique when I got home, but my mom stopped me mid-sentence. "Ralph called," she said, "and he's having a Fourth of July party tomorrow night at his house. Both you and Angelique are invited. Oh, and be sure to wear costumes that have something to do with American history."

"He invited the French kid?"

"Well, he couldn't very well have left out your guest!"

As I walked up the stairs to my room, I started thinking how well Ralph had recovered from the Dairy Queen fiasco. Maybe a guy needs to be slapped in the face every once in a while.

Despite all my explanations, Angelique didn't quite understand the whole "party" thing.

"Party. There's gonna be a party at Ralph's place and we're invited. You know, party. Fiesta!"

"It is when, the party?"

"Tomorrow. Tomorrow night at six. And it's for the Fourth of July, you know, our day of independence."

"No fourteenz of July?"

"Not in this country! It's sort of like a costume party—that means you dress up and put on clothes you wouldn't normally wear."

"On fourz of July?"

"Yeah." I was getting pretty exasperated.

"I zink I have an idea. I go to party as Mari-lyn Monroe. You know—'Appy Birzday Meester President...'" She was singing pretty loudly.

"Okay, okay, whatever," I said, trying to shut her up. "Just as long as you can find some costume." I walked out of the room and left her alone.

When Angelique woke up the next afternoon, we went through the pancake routine with a lot of fanfare and then ran upstairs to get ready for the party. I threw together a cowboy thing for myself, complete with a mustache, an enormous cowboy hat, a plastic rifle and a pair of my little brother's cowboy boots. I went to check on Angelique after I had finished gluing on the right side of my mustache. She was on the bed, tying the straps of a white spandex halter-top around her neck. When she'd finished, she tightened her silver sandals and leaned over to the mirror to check her makeup: blue sparkling eye shadow, tomato-red lipstick, super-thick layer of mascara. She made smooching noises with her lips in front of the mirror. "You like?" she asked, turning around abruptly. She was wearing the shortest, tightest shorts I'd ever seen and it was obvious she wasn't wearing a bra. I knew right then she'd be the cleavage queen of the party.

My mom looked really shocked when Angelique came down the stairs, her chest bobbing up and down every step of the way. "Wouldn't you like to wear a shawl, dear?" she asked, pulling an old floral-printed thing out of the closet that looked like it must have come from the seventies. The French kid said no, she would be fine, and we left my mother standing there, aghast.

I had just gotten my license and I was pretty psyched to show off my driving skills in front of Angelique. Ralph's house was only five blocks away, but it looked a lot cooler to arrive in a car. All the guys whistled when we walked in, and Ralph grabbed the French kid by the arm to show her off to his friends.

"Hey, Ange-el, wanna screw?" Ralph asked.

Angelique giggled and said "no zank yooo" as if he had just offered her a soft drink.

The party went okay, I guess. There were red, white and blue streamers hung on all of the walls, and a couple of guys were wearing Statue of Liberty masks. Angelique was certainly princess of the evening in her Marilyn Monroe costume; after a few minutes, everyone seemed to forget that I had brought her in the first place. A million guys tried to hook up with her at the same time, but she just stood by the punch bowl and kept pouring the red stuff in her plastic cup. After a while, she loosened up and left the punch bowl table for the dance floor. I could tell she was drunk when she started speaking French and wouldn't say a word of English to anybody. She went completely ballistic when Ralph put on the song "Voulez-Vous Coucher Avec Moi, Ce Soir?" I figured it was time for a quick exit when she started dancing on top of the table.

"Come on, Angelique, it's time to go!" I yanked her down from the table, thanked Ralph for the party and jammed her in the backseat of the Volvo. My cowboy boots had given me these awful blisters so I took them off to drive, right about the time Angelique started to sing. She started singing Ricky Martin's "Livin' la Vida Loca" mixed in with some crazy-sounding French lyrics.

"I want to take my clothes off and go *danser* in ze rrrain," she howled from the backseat. When Angelique screamed a sentence in French that sounded like "turn off the oven, there's a camel in the ice cream!" my nerves got pretty frazzled and I drove right through a stoplight.

I had no idea she was cooking up something even more disastrous. Still sprawled out in the back of the car, the kid took off one of her five-inch-platform silver sandals and hurled it out the car window. I slammed on the brakes with my bare foot when I heard the thud and prayed there was no one on the street. But by some fluke, the shoe landed two feet away from an unmarked police car parked on the side of the road. When the blue blinking lights suddenly went on, I wanted to strangle Angelique right there on the spot. How could she have gotten us into this mess in just five blocks?

"Remain in the vehicle with your hands on the wheel," the policeman blasted over his megaphone as we pulled over to the sidewalk. Holding the sandal in his hand, he walked around the car to observe it from all angles. He paused for a moment when he saw Angelique still singing her French songs and lying stretched out in the back. The cop didn't look pleased to see my peeling fake mustache and cowboy boots in the passenger seat. He glared at me.

"Get out of the vehicle."

I took my hands off the wheel and poked Angelique with the toe of a cowboy boot before opening the car door.

"Get your ass out of the car," I whispered to her. She wouldn't budge, so I got out alone.

"License?"

I reached in the pocket of my jeans and pulled out my driver's license. He studied my photograph for a good thirty seconds.

"Did you know drunk driving is against the law, Ms. Brooks?" he asked, holding a Breathalyzer test to my face. I told him I wasn't drunk and walked a straight line to prove it.

"Then why is this silver shoe in my hand?" he asked sarcastically. Tapping my finger on the window, I pointed to Angelique.

"It's not mine. It's hers."

"And did you learn in Drivers' Education, Ms. Brooks, that it is illegal to go through a red light?"

I nodded. "I'm sorry, sir."

"And you know how else you broke the law? You drove this vehicle without wearing shoes. And it is illegal, I repeat *illegal* to drive barefoot!"

I looked down at my blistered feet and wiggled my toes a little bit.

"Come with me, we're going to the station."

Angelique was still lying in the backseat singing as loudly as ever. I would have ordinarily been thrilled at the opportunity to drag her out of the car by the ankles, but it didn't seem too exciting with a cop standing right there. Once she had regained her balance, the kid leaned on the car door and abruptly stopped singing.

"Bonjourrrrr mon amourrr," she said to the cop, rolling the "r's" in the back of her mouth as if she were gargling mouthwash. "'Appy Birzday Meester President...'Appy Birzday to yooooou."

We arrived at the station at two o'clock in the morning. Angelique conked out on one of the benches while the cop was having a long conversation with my mom on the phone—long because he had to explain the situation at least four times before my mom grasped what was going on. Fifteen minutes later she arrived at the station wearing my dad's old shirt and the same shawl she had tried to give to Angelique. Her hair was all over the place. While my mom negotiated all the legal stuff with the policeman, she cast vicious glances at me (Angelique was still dead to the world). I thought she was going to spank us when we got home, but she just picked up the phone and tried to call Air France. She didn't have much luck at 3:00 AM; the real conversations with the airlines began the next morning before breakfast.

Angelique woke up grumpy and hungover with not much recollection of what had happened the night before. Though she didn't seem thrilled with the idea of packing up all her stuff and clearing out of the house in fifteen minutes, I think the kid was happy to return to France and bid Richmond farewell. The summer hadn't exactly been a lesson in French etiquette, but I didn't mind too much, so long as the pancake ordeal was over.

When I moved back into my old room the day she left, I thought Angelique was gone from my life forever, but as I opened my closet door to hang my clothes where hers had been, a ghastly odor slapped me across the face. I gagged and waited a good two minutes before diving back in the closet to discover the cause of the stench. Sure enough, the kid had left a token for us to remember her by: a small ziplock plastic bag that smelled like vomit and rotten milk put together. I picked up the bag with my thumb and index finger and examined its contents: inside, there was a slab of French cheese covered in a thick layer of blue and white mold. Apparently the custom's official hadn't taken her entire stash of food; my dad could have his gourmet dish after all.

Sascha Braunig
Family Reunion

My aunts
Wizened booze-hounds
Drain their glasses
And sing drily,
Cracked, black-haired
And garish.
They are four birds with smoky halos.
Their failed marriages and delinquent
Children
Trail behind them like mascara.
I sit amazed at their wrinkled
Drunken glory.
My cousins smoke pot
Ask me "How was your trip?"
My uncles
All hockey and nicotine
Have no dignity.
They can only shift their sad sacks of flesh around
While my aunts croon
Cackle and wheeze.
They know the score.

Caitlin Doyle
Dublin, 1946

My father stole a boat
when he was twelve years old.
He swam out to the tiny island
of a rich man
and pulled the boat home.
The neighborhood helped him
hoist it above their heads,
skinny legs sticking out under
Jaysus—did you ever see a boat walking?
Boys pitching and painting
until the long grass waved down the sun
and each boy went home John Wayne
into the dusk.
My father pitched until the stars
widened their eyes at the ship forming in his hands—
that was before the world said
Put out your hands.
Like a child receiving a present
he turned his palms up—
the strap came down
not a sound in the room
the strap came down
and down and down and down,
blood beaten into the stars.
My father left school,
gave the boat to some younger boys,
became an electrician's apprentice.

He taught his hands to sense
the dangerous wires,
the silent killers
that could fry a man
at any moment.

Lindsay Horlor
Episodes One To Ten
(For Mom)

When you die,
I want your wedding ring.
Something to remember
the memories of a family,
that was once a family, all together
in one house.
Six people, though our lives, nothing
like an episode of *The Brady Bunch*.
In real life, Carol is dying
of cancer and she cheated
on Mike Brady.
There weren't any family trips
to Hawaii,
and Marsha has an ulcer.
Like a game of Jenga,
we are small,
wooden blocks, falling
one piece, then the next.
I'll wear the ring on a chain
around my neck,
clutch it when I get nervous.
Think of you,
then visit your grave.
Rest a white lily on
the dark soil.
The day you die,
it will rain. Black clouds
and lightning will hog the sky.

We loved those days the most,
no electricity,
the television screen black.

Sarah Hudson
Ngwelezana

I have to wear a dress
the day Dad takes me to Ngwelezana hospital.

We drive in the gates
past benches of people waiting
for the Volkswagen vans that are black taxis.
They drink orange soda
say their goodbyes.

We walk through a dim corridor
stop to read notices on walls:
the morning's death tally is 5
bodies will be kept for 10 days only.

"One in three," the superintendent comments
as we move through the wards.
I hesitate to play with the children on the floor
count them first, wondering.

An elderly woman writhes, her sheets stained with blood
one dark breast exposed.
She reaches for my mother
white, blond angel standing near.

In the courtyard
a man crouches on a rock
his bare upper body covered
in flies and mosquitoes.
He is trying to heal his open sores
with sunlight.

Before getting into the car
I stand with my pale mother and
look back at Ngwelezana hospital
buried deep among
the rolling hills of sugar cane
where Africa bleeds to death.

Dan Shumuk
Porch Light

Midnight is the crack
in the vinyl seat of Dad's pickup
the green foam underneath
threatening to split
down to unfriendly springs
The ones seen on TV
after car fires

Midnight is a long way from home
a tropical storm that would
soon become a hurricane
He's Late has grown
into *Where the Hell Is He*
Only 16 storms like this one
ever seen this century

Midnight is three lines
that blur in between Orion the hunter
and Taurus the bull
Smack dab in the middle of a black hole
even the light of day can't escape

After midnight is the man that hides
in the porch light until morning
His eyes light up and follow you
up the steps
as if you lived in Hollywood
as if you were a star

Todd
First Time

My mother always told me
when it happened we would
have dinner on Broadway
or go shopping and pick something out
in the women's section.
Halloween, 1994:
twelve years old, two long braids
clear skin, bony as hell
frigid air and firecrackers
the smell of burning leaves.
I was kicking chestnuts,
cigarette glowing,
a weighty bag of candy,
rejected from doorsteps because I looked too old
in the eyes of disapproving baby boomers.
Home again, pulling down my underwear,
incredulous before the sudden, intense red
on clean cotton.
My mother was playing David Lanz on her piano,
a sad piece.
I dangled my underwear for her to see. She released the keys,
went quiet,
took the bones of my fingers
and kissed them.

Monika Lee
Dizzy

Everything was upside down and spinning. He had me by the ankles and flipped me into the air as if I were a pancake. Faster and faster he went, the ceiling beginning to blur into walls, into blue carpet where I'd spilt apple juice that morning. When he put me down, I couldn't tell one thing from another. I sat with my head in my hands trying to focus on my pink Velcro sneakers.

"Okay, enough of that. I don't want to make you sick!" my grandpa announced in his booming Norwegian accent, each word echoing off the walls of the tiny apartment, as if we stood at the edge of a deep canyon.

"Let's play a game, teach me something," I whined, tugging at his pant leg.

"Okay, I know a good one. Repeat after me. Toy boat," Grandpa said. "Toy boat," I said as I climbed into his lap.

"Again, toy boat, toy boat, toy boat," he said, faster now.

"Toy boat. Grandpa, this is too easy," I complained.

"No, no. You say it over and over again and go faster and faster. Try," he demanded.

"Toy boat, toy boat, toy boat, toy boat, toy boat!" I shouted, making him laugh so hard his belly moved in and out, bouncing me off his knee. I ended up rolling along the floor, holding my sides so they wouldn't burst.

He wiped a tear from the corner of his eye, then leaned down to whisper in my ear, "You were rushing. Sometimes we try to rush things and they end up all mixed up. You went so fast the words didn't make sense and you said something you didn't mean."

This is what I remember when my mother tells me my grandparents are getting divorced. I don't cry, but I keep imagining them lying in bed together before they turned the lights out. They are playing this game, chanting over and over, "Love, love, love."

Carly Lutzmann
Every Thursday Brandi Wears an Evening Gown to Class

The first time Brandi wore an evening gown to class we were all surprised. It was a cloudy Thursday afternoon and we were about to take our weekly test—this week the subject was algebra. As the teacher passed out the tests, Brandi ran into the classroom, layers of tulle and sequins dragging on the linoleum behind her.

"Sorry I'm late," she said breathlessly, taking a seat at the front of the class. "I had a little fashion emergency."

"Apparently so," someone muttered under her breath, but Brandi just smiled. She started writing the test, two desks ahead of me and one to my right. It was so hard to concentrate on the equations when there was a puffball of ivory satin and netting so close by, brushing against her chair every time she moved her legs. I noticed the other students were distracted too. Cindy continually tapped her pencil against the desk, and Brian kept shaking his head.

On Monday, when we got the tests back, Brandi aced it. I barely got a C. For the next three months she wore the evening gown to class every Thursday, and she aced every test we took. It didn't matter whether it was polynomials or trigonometry, when Brandi put on the dress she became a math genius.

In June, when final exams rolled around, our class decided to cash in on Brandi's bright idea. We spent more time shopping for gowns and tuxedos than doing the review questions. Getting our shoes dyed became a bigger priority than understanding geometry, and cummerbunds seemed the perfect solution to calculus. Few students opened their textbooks, and when they finally did it was to press a flower from their corsage.

My friends and I rented a limo for exam day, and when we pulled up to the curb we saw a sea of formal wear. Empire waists and fishtail hems, tuxedo pants and bow ties were everywhere. When the bell rang we headed toward our math class, armed with pencils to match our dresses and erasers in complementary pastel tones.

Our teacher passed out the tests, her face betraying no sense of surprise she was feeling. She explained the rules to us—keep your eyes on your own test, when you're finished raise your hand—and told us to begin. I opened my booklet and read the first question. My throat tightened. I flipped through the book to find an easy question, one to warm up with, but they may as well have been written in Yiddish. I started to sweat.

At that moment the door opened. Brandi rushed in, a cloud of electric pink and orange. Only this time it wasn't an evening gown—it was a ski suit. On this hot June morning she had chosen a down-filled, fleece-lined jacket with thermally insulated pants and heavy boots. She even had a pair of goggles over her eyes.

"Sorry," we heard her say to our teacher, "but I had another little emergency." And from the looks of it, so did we.

Nicholas Melling
Philemon

The family is sitting at the kitchen table. For the most part, they are motionless. Certainly they are silent. The chamber has the air of a hospital waiting room, both in the grimness of its inhabitants and the sterility of their surroundings.

They have almost finished their dinner: meat loaf and mashed potatoes. It has been Tuesday's fare as long as anyone can remember. By now the family sees the meal as a perennial menace, like the weekly visits of Jehovah's Witness ambassadors. But changing the routine would mean inventing a replacement, so they stoically consume the dismal food without leaving too much on their plates.

There are three of them at the table tonight. There have been three since the departure of Joanna, who fled for a land where meat loaf does not come back to haunt the house every Tuesday. There is also a dog, a black Lab who lies under the table. He has been with them for many years and no longer hopes for edible gifts to come his way.

The father of the house is a squat man with large glasses encircling small piggy eyes. He is the only member of the family still eating: a task which he does with great speed and skill, having had much practice.

His companion is sitting across the table from him. It is she who has concocted the meat loaf, though she has eaten little of it. She sits with her elbow on the table and her chin in her hand, regarding the rest of the family impassively.

Their son is half sitting, half lying in his chair. His feet rest on the body of the dog under him. He is waiting for the word of dismissal from either of his parents, one of the few disciplinary habits that has stood the test of time. No one can leave the table until everyone is finished eating. In the meantime, he amuses himself by tossing peas one by one into a water glass. Although this task requires more athletic effort than the son is usually willing to exert, it has the pleasant side effect of annoying his father, who regards all games involving food as sacrilegious.

Discerning his son's intent, the father retaliates by slowing his pace of eating. He begins to chew his food with feline care, leaving long pauses between each swallow.

During one of these breaks, he asks his son, "Do you want any more meat loaf?" There is a gloating gleam in his eye.

The son turns the glass on its side, presenting a horizontal target. He is now flicking the peas into it. "I think your need is greater than mine, Dad."

"Then I'll have another piece. And could you pass the peas?" There is triumph in the father's tone.

Undaunted, the son begins to pass the peas, one at a time, to his father. Most do land on his plate; the son has become an expert.

Abruptly, the silent mother speaks. "You can go." Her husband bestows on her the look of a betrayed child. Their son gives them both a warm smile, a victorious general accepting surrender. He slides off his chair and out of the room, followed by the black Lab.

The father puts the meat loaf he has taken back onto the serving plate. He and his wife sit in silence.

"Cliff Allen's father died today," he ventures at last. "He had a heart attack and died."

"He was in his nineties," his wife observes.

"In fifty years, we'll be in our nineties."

The wife is silent. She cannot argue with this.

"In forty years, we'll be in our eighties." The husband has found a reliable vehicle for conversation.

The wife stands up. Left without an audience for his predictions, her husband does the same. Dinner is over.

The son is in his room. He is reading a book. This is an unusual pastime for him, especially in summer when he regards every academic activity as a waste of time. There are very few activities, in fact, that he does not see in this light. His dog is sitting beside him on the bed. The dog views sedentary activity as a waste of time, but is far too polite to tell this to the boy. They waste twenty minutes together, in silence.

The phone rings. The boy waits until the third tone, then answers. "Speaking," he says.

"What?" says his caller.

"Speaking."

There is a pause.

"Is your mom or dad home?" the caller asks.

"I don't know."

Another pause.

"Maybe I'll call back later," the caller says at last.

"Maybe you will," the boy agrees. The caller hangs up.

He returns to his book. Rarely does the boy read in a linear fashion; he chooses paragraphs at random from various pages. Right now, he is reading from somewhere in the middle of the book:

July 17th today we went to see Egerdon Castle which doesn't actually exist anymore but is still a great tourist attraction and it's really quite comical to see these crowds of people gaping in awe at the grassy hill on which egerdon castle used to stand before it was destroyed by thoughtless barbarians a thousand years ago but i guess it wasn't too funny because my whole goddam family was there gaping with the best of them actually i lied when i said the castle doesn't exist anymore because it does in part there's almost three feet of wall still standing and they've encircled it with a chainlink fence just in case the thoughtless barbarians might be lurking outside waiting for a chance to finish the

job anyway after we'd finished staring reverently at the wall
inside the chain link fence we got in the car and drove away
the way we'd came and that pretty much sums up my day.

It is not the first time the boy has indulged in perusing Joanna's journal. It is more interesting than most of the other books he reads, although he himself is rarely mentioned in it as any more than a part of Joanna's goddam family.

The boy's parents are washing the dishes. Such grim work invariably breeds grim conversation.

"I think I'm going to die before I reach my nineties," the husband confesses.

"Probably," agrees his wife.

"I think you will too," he adds sharply. Even prophets are not always compassionate.

"Perhaps we'll die at the same time," his wife suggests.

The husband contemplates this notion for a while. Sadly, his meditation distracts him from his earthly duty of drying dishes, and the drying process grinds to a halt.

"No," he says at last. "I don't think that will happen." He does not explain his reasoning. Prophecies rarely come with explanations.

"We might both turn into trees at the same time," proposes his wife. "We might be suddenly changed into trees by a benevolent god."

"Or we might die of heart attacks. Lots of people die of heart attacks these days."

"It isn't impossible to suddenly turn into a tree. It has been known to happen."

"And there's always cancer. You'll probably die of cancer if you don't die of a heart attack."

"What was the guy's name? The guy who got turned into a tree with his wife?"

"You know, I think I'm going to get cancer *and* a heart attack. I'll have cancer for a while and bam! Heart attack will get me."

"Philemon and Baucis."

"What?"

"Philemon and Baucis. Neither one wanted to die before the other, so some god turned them into trees."

"Into dead trees?"

"No, living trees."

"So they would still have to die of something. And one would probably die before the other. The *god* didn't really solve their problem." There is a pause. Such canny observations do not often originate from the husband.

"They were probably chain-sawed to pieces in a most painful manner," says the wife. "The *god* probably turned them into trees and then took a chain saw to them for fun."

"I'll bet he didn't cut both of them down at once, either," says the husband. "I bet he cut down one, and then waited, and *then* cut down the other one."

"Probably," the wife agrees.

The son has entered the kitchen. He has advanced quietly, and only now do his parents become aware of him.

"Why don't you help us with the dishes?" his mother asks. The question is meant to be rhetorical.

"Because I'm allergic to water," the son replies. The father stops drying. He is contemplating his son's comment.

"Then why are you always taking showers?" demands his father triumphantly, returning to his drying.

"Because I am a masochist." The drying stops again. The mother, used to such contradictions, continues washing.

"Do you remember Egerdon Castle?" the son asks suddenly.

The parents are somewhat taken aback. Their son has always carried himself with a studied indifference toward all things, making his asking of a question quite startling. "Not specifically," says his mother. "We saw some castles when we were in England."

"Why?" asks his father.

The son's interest in the matter is abruptly extinguished. "Nothing. I was just reading something…it mentioned Egerdon Castle."

The fact that the son has asked a question is a surprise to his parents. But the shock of knowing that this question stemmed from something he read—this is a blow that threatens to drive the father to the heart attack he has prophesied.

"What did you read?" his father shouts. A book with the ability to arouse interest in his son is surely a book possessing supernatural powers.

The son decides not to tell his parents. He is given to such arbitrary withholding of information, especially when it serves to annoy his father. Instead he opts for a change of subject.

"Someone called just now. They wanted to know if either of you were home."

"I imagine you told them we weren't," says his mother.

"I didn't say one way or the other. But they didn't seem to want to talk to you. They just wanted to know if you were home."

"That could have been an important call!" shouts the father, bent on defeating his son in a battle of decibels.

"Should I call the person back and assure them that both of you are, indeed, safe and sound at home?"

The father has become enraged. His state of mind is having a happy effect upon the dishes, which he is drying furiously.

The phone rings. The father charges to the cordless on the table.

"What?" he yells into the receiver.

"Why can't anyone in your family just say hello?"

"What?"

"My father died today, and all you people do is torment me."
The father is baffled. He remains silent.

"You were home all along, weren't you? You prick!"

The father continues his silence. The caller hangs up.

It is then that the father receives the heart attack he has been expecting all evening.

The mother will say later that the evening's misfortunes were brought about by unhappy circumstance. The father, from his bed in the hospital, will blame his son. The son, who is immune to guilt, will blame his father's diet. But no one will think to blame the *god*, chain saw in hand, who has been biding his time for just such an opportunity.

Michael Mulley
Bedrock

It's the name. It seems to her that it's always the name. The craggy-faced cashier in this Northern Ontario general store has been staring at her disapprovingly, and sure enough has just asked her to spell her name. Now she's making a great show of being confused by it: people from around here don't have names like Titania.

"Is that Romanian, dear?" the woman asks.

"No," Titania answers curtly, fully realizing that she's just confirmed the woman's worst suspicions and been labeled as another of the Rains, Harmonys and Moonbeams that visit every so often, city people wandering the dirt roads, searching for the place that offers spiritual glory as well as good cappuccino. Titania has always wondered about her name. What, she wonders, had caused her mother to name her so creatively, and why, in her entire remembered life, had she never seen a trace of this creativity again? Strangers always assume Titania is the child of hippie parents, raised barefoot amid love and nature. And when she thinks about the pinched shoe that was her childhood, she often creates alternate parents for herself; if only that spontaneity and flair in her mother hadn't been suppressed so quickly.

After buying her bug spray and chili, things she becomes dependent on when traveling, Titania walks around the store and waits for her husband. A collection of decorated eggs is glued to the ceiling, fishing lures are attached to every wall and wooden geese stare menacingly from every aisle. There is a corner of tables, couches and chessboards, but the corner is empty and covered in a thick layer of dust. She wonders who comes here. Lawyers looking for more and more distant cottages? The few locals, returning every day at the same hour?

Lost travelers like themselves? Of course, she would until recently have wondered the same about a place like Saskatoon— under a million people? It doesn't exist?—but here she is now, being dragged across the country en route to Saskatoon, herded like a sheep at the whim of her husband and his ever-relocating job. Saskatoon! She can hardly believe it. The prairie, the bread-basket, the home, she hears, of the World's Largest Perogy. At least there's that: they won't be going hungry.

Her head snaps up. Her husband, Hal, is calling her from outside and she quickly leaves the store to join him. She has been dreaming. *The first sign of senility*, he calls it. *The only way to avoid a senile husband*, she usually replies. Saying this used to offend him, but it's now only a weary ritual.

They're back in the car; he starts the car; they're back on the road. They had taken a wrong turn earlier and only realized their mistake two gravel-road-hours later. They've turned back now and have just reached the main highway again, the car coated in a thick white dust. The car is an old Mazda, rusty but tenacious, the family pet. They have spent the last week on the road, and it is now both a home and a companion. They call it Magda, speak to it in a Hungarian accent. Conversation seems easy with the car.

With each other, they play games. Today, it is Geography.

"Delaware," he says.

"Ecuador," she answers.

"Reno."

"Orillia."

"Aix."

"You can't say that."

"What?"

"You can't say that," she repeats, her voice flat. "It's Aix-en-Provence. Aix is only half a name."

"It's a full name. I've been there, I've stayed in the hotels, I've eaten the cheese. It's Aix."

121

"I don't care what you call it. On the map, it's Aix-en-Provence. That's what counts. I've got a map somewhere, find it, I'll show you."

"Fine!" he yells.

"What?" she asks, surprised.

"Fine!" he yells again. "Fine! Ajax!"

And she leans back and thinks, and neither of them speaks until an hour has passed and they have reached their turnoff. This has happened before: after a few minutes, one of them mentions Appomattox or Phoenix or the Bronx and the other stays silent for ages, trying to remember the name of that city in China—Xanwen? Xinhuang? and wishing, stupidly, for Xanadu.

They take their turnoff and drive quickly along the empty streets of Sault Ste. Marie. Downtown is a maze of lanes and one-way streets, built to handle an onslaught of traffic it seems to never have received. Now, on a calm summer evening, it is empty, only streetlamps and the occasional quiet restaurant lighting up the pristine streets. From every corner tourist signs blare: *World's Largest Locks! See the Locks in Action! Locks, Locks, Locks!* Titania can't believe it. How bored or boring do you have to be, she wonders, to vacation at the locks, to watch the water go up and then, after a suspenseful pause, go back down?

"Looks like the locks are closed," says Hal.

Titania hopes that this is only small talk, an attempt to start a conversation. She has lived with him for almost three years now; she would have known by now if he were a lock man. She doesn't answer. She's not sure she wants to hear the reply. Besides, they're about to reach their destination, the bed-and-breakfast where they'll spend the night. It's called Pineview, and the view is indeed of a pine tree: thick, squat and balding. The building is short and concrete, spread-eagled across the cluttered lawn and painted a particularly dreary shade of beige. They walk down the dirt path to the door, knock and try the handle. It's not locked. Titania opens the door and is greeted by a thigh.

A single thigh, a large thigh, an impressive thigh. As she opens the door fully, she sees that it's part of a big poster, hanging right beside the coatrack, of a thigh-dominated body, which according to the caption belongs to Buck "The Ram" Armstrong.

A short, chubby couple comes running toward them. "Hi," says the woman, breathlessly, "I'm Bobbi and this is my husband Brett. I've just finished cleaning your room, it's right down this way." Bobbi leads them down a carpeted hallway and opens the door to their room. The furniture is simple and unremarkable but on the walls are several posters of wrestling stars, glaring angrily at them from all corners.

Hal coughs. "I've noticed that you have a large number of these posters here," he says, polite and awkward. "Is this a personal interest, or—" But Titania has already walked into the attached bathroom and closed the door. She doesn't hear the end of the question. Some things, she thinks, are better left unanswered. It has been an early morning and a long day, and she is tired. She washes and changes quickly and then climbs immediately into bed, pulling the covers up as far as they will go. Above her, on the sloping ceiling, a brawny, oiled man looks down at her angrily, fists raised, and pins her to the bed, forcing her into an uneasy sleep.

The next morning they wake early, while it's still dark. There is ground to cover, time to make. They pack and clean quietly, pay for the night with money left on top of the TV and head outside. They're surprised to see Bobbi and Brett in the kitchen, fully awake at this hour. Bobbi is cooking breakfast— eggs, sausages, ham, more sausages, something that looks terrifyingly like lard—but Titania can't trust herself not to vomit and, despite Hal's hungry grunts, tells Bobbi that they'd love to but they really do have to go. Bobbi decides to be affectionate and gives her a smothering hug and then they're on their way.

The locks are still closed as they drive out of town. Neither mentions them.

They are soon out in the open country, forty miles from the nearest donut. It is dawn, the road is empty except for the occasional trucker, and the trees and cliffs and water are serene and still, arranged in perfect sleeping symmetry. It is wonderful and forces them to stare. They can't stop themselves from speaking; they babble in awe, their words rushed yet pointless.

"Over there, look, beneath that waterfall…"

"It's so green, so…"

"And over there, the lake. It's so big, isn't it? Goes on forever…"

And they continue on like this until the road turns and moves inland, and they are silent, only Magda's quiet hum resonating in their ears.

"It's the world's largest," says Hal, pointing to the side of the road. It's a statue of a goose, and it is indeed large. Ugly, but large. Titania grunts in assent. This is what isolation and vast spaces do to people, she thinks. There's the largest perogy, the largest locks, and, according to their guidebook, they missed seeing (alas!) the World's Largest Nickel in Sudbury. And so, because visitors didn't have enough large things at their disposal, the little town of Wawa decided to build itself a goose. Why something large? Why a goose? Why not Wawa Medieval Village, Wawa Museum of Baby Talk, something? Is lack of size and sophistication not enough for small towns, do they have to embarrass themselves with large ugly statues as well?

But she doesn't say any of this. Instead she grunts, and that grunt lasts them the next twenty minutes.

They make good time; they cover good ground. By nine o'clock at night, they are in Thunder Bay. The bay is filthy and there is no thunder. Their bed-and-breakfast for the night is slightly out of town, perched on top of a hill. It is called the Aeschylus. The brochure gives a definition: a Greek tragedian. A stupid name. She walks up the path and rings the doorbell—a bell, literally, with a string. The door is opened seconds later by a tall, old man, about sixty she'd guess. He is dressed in a shiny pressed jacket and holds a cane in his hand. All that's needed to complete the costume, she thinks, is a monocle.

"Hello! Come in, come in. My name is Lucius. You've just come from Wawa?" He glances disapprovingly at their mud-splattered car in the driveway.

"No," says Hal, "Sault Ste. Marie."

"Oh! That *is* a long way. You must be extremely tired."

"Nah, not really," says Titania, intentionally mumbling and slurring in response to his enunciation.

"I am," says Hal.

"Well, by ten thirty I'm fast asleep. Should you be going out, you'll need a key; one is in your room."

"Wonderful," says Titania, though it sounds more like "Wunnerful."

Lucius leads them to their room—it has photographs of statues from the Parthenon on the wall, really quite nice, though it smells mouldy—and departs.

"You're not going to go to bed now, are you?" asks Titania.

"Well, yeah, I am."

"It's only nine thirty. And we've been in a small boxy car all day. We can't do this. This is living like cattle."

"Maybe, but very tired cattle. Anyway, we're in Thunder Bay. What's there to do here? They have Tim Horton's in Saskatoon too, you know."

"I don't know. Wander, explore, something, anything."

"Sorry."

"If you don't come, I'll go myself."

He is already on the bed, his shirt half off and a resigned look on his face. He sighs. "Be careful then. And be back soon."

She picks up the key and walks outside. She has no idea where she's going. He was right: it is Thunder Bay. To the best of her knowledge, it doesn't even have the world's largest anything. She sees lights to her left and sets off in that direction.

Once she arrives, she sees that the lights belong to what looks like a faux-English pub called the Partridge Arms. She walks in. The British charm is limited to the sign outside: inside, it's just a bar, dingy and green, lit by flickering neon on the walls. She finds herself a table in the corner and orders herself a beer. She begins to nurse it. Why, she wonders to herself, is Hal so bloody boring? He's dragging her to Saskatoon. He never says anything of interest. He drives all day and then goes to sleep. Her mother approves of him. Could she have made a worse decision? But she tries not to dwell on these thoughts. They are angry, she tells herself, they are painful. And besides, she isn't the dwelling type. She sighs and takes another sip of beer. She needs it.

She hears some whispering behind her, loud and slightly drunken. It's a group of young men, and from the corner of her eye she can see that one of them is looking at her intently. He looks about thirty, brown hair, brown eyes, cute. As soon as he sees her looking at him, he turns away. He looks nice, she thinks. A bit young, but there's nothing wrong with that. And frankly, right now she needs a bit of excitement, a bit of romance. But how can she be thinking this? He has only looked at her! She returns to her beer but then hears the creak of a chair moving and footsteps. She looks over; he has gotten up and is walking. At first, she thinks that he's walking toward the bar, but she soon sees that he's walking toward her, moving awkwardly. He is holding his hands tightly to his sides and staring at his shoes. He has a bit of a limp. These shuffling motions make him look almost like a child, and she immediately feels affectionate toward him. He reminds her of someone too—someone from long ago, a rare happy childhood memory—but she can't quite remember who. He really is quite good-looking. She realizes that she is staring at him as he comes up to her table, but she doesn't care.

"Hi," he says, looking down shyly.

"Hi," she answers warmly. "I'm Titania." She motions for him to sit down beside her. He doesn't, though, and stays standing over her.

"Hi," he repeats. "My name is…" He is still looking down, and he's stammering. He's terminally shy, but she finds this endearing. She widens her smile and again motions for him to sit down. He pauses and then looks up, his face now firm. "My name's Fred Flintstone, and I can make your bedrock."

His face stays firm for about a second and then he breaks into loud, raucous, mean laughter. Titania is stunned. She forces herself to laugh—in the shock of the moment, she can think of nothing else to do—though her eyes are blurry. By the time she wipes her eyes and can see again, he is gone, back in his group. They are all laughing together, a group of faces equally loud, raucous and mean.

So far, she has had only half a beer. But now, she is determined: she will get drunk, and fast. She finishes the beer in seconds and orders vodka. She doesn't enjoy it—like a flame, like a blade—but she is very much determined, and she drinks quickly. Forty minutes later, she gets up and leaves. The streets are dark and empty, and she begins to walk in the opposite direction from the bed-and-breakfast. Her thoughts are not clear, but she knows that she expects to find something out here in the cold night air, to learn something about life. She is looking for guidance, for truth, for meaning, for direction.

She finds litter. A surprising amount and variety of it: wrappers, bottles, notes, children's toys, crumpled pages out of a Harlequin romance, a pristine glass paperweight with fake snow that swirls around a miniature replica of the World's Largest Goose. The things she finds are really quite interesting, and she lurches around unsteadily for hours collecting. Several hours later, when her arms are full, her back hurts and her mind is slightly clearer, she decides to return to the bed-and-breakfast.

It is five o'clock by the time she gets back. She dumps her pile of litter by the door and walks into the room. Hal is awake, curled on the bed, his head between his knees. As she walks in, he tilts his head up and a look of sudden anger and relief washes over his face. At first he says nothing. Titania walks over to the table and takes off her earrings.

"Where have you been?" he says softly.

"Out." Her words are surly and mumbled.

"Where have you been?"

"Out. To a pub. Then around, walking."

"Do you know what time it is? Do you know how long you've been out? Do you know how long I've been waiting?" His voice is calmly flat.

She doesn't answer.

"You're drunk."

This time, she answers. "No. I *was* drunk, but not anymore, damn it."

He is standing now. "What the hell has happened to you? Are you the same person? You've just spent a night drunk, walking the streets of small town Ontario. Are you possessed?"

Her thoughts are not clear; all she can think of is anger. "What's happened to *me*? It's you who've changed: mechanical, silent, boring, going to live in Saskatchewan!"

"Okay. Enough."

"No! You can't shut me up!" She feels her chest tighten. "This isn't a game. This isn't Geography. You can't use the letter X and silence me."

He has begun to pace. He turns away from her. "Believe me, I can. It's you who've spent a night on the streets, it's you who've run off. You have no right to be angry at me. Shut up."

There is a long pause. "Motherfucker." This is the only word she says before turning and leaving, legs unsteady and eyes blurred once more. She slams the door to their room; she slams the door to the house; she kicks the stones on the balcony

128

as hard as she can. As she runs down the street, she whispers to herself, the words slowly losing any meaning and forming a mantra: *Motherfucker. Motherfucker.*

Back on the early-morning streets of Thunder Bay, she wanders angrily. She eats donuts, just cooked and still warm. She does not enjoy them. She wanders some more. At eight in the morning, she is back once again at the Aeschylus. Hal is in the car, waiting. She opens the door and climbs in. He starts the car, steps on the gas and drives away.

They make good time. They make great time. Four hours later, they are in Manitoba. Nobody has spoken, and the air between them is thick, tense, ready to crack. The car is running out of gas. They stop at a gas station. It is self-serve; Hal gets out and starts pumping.

They are on the prairie now. The gas station is on a raised cement platform, four or five feet above the ground. The land is flat, completely flat—she hadn't thought it could be true—and she has a commanding view over the landscape. The fields are full of canola: bright, blazing and yellow. The dirt roads form a precise grid on the sides of the farms, and at seemingly even intervals a truck drives slowly along, obscured by the vast and swirling cloud of dust that it kicks up. The sky is large and empty, covering the ground like a blanket. It is, she admits, beautiful. And considering that she's going to be living here, it had better be beautiful, she had bloody well better like it.

Hal returns to the car. They leave the station and turn off the highway, onto a dirt road that is supposed to be a shortcut. Finally, Hal breaks the silence. "You know, Lucius didn't go to bed early last night."

Titania doesn't answer.

"He stayed up and watched a movie. His room was right beneath ours; I could hear every word. It was called *The Harder They Come*. The story of Nalgena, an innocent Tahitian woman who loses her innocence five minutes into the movie."

129

Now, Titania has lifted her head and begun to smile. "You mean…"

"Oh yes. Very much so." They are chuckling. Suddenly, Titania bursts into peals of laughter. She is pointing madly out the window, her whole arm shaking.

"Look! Look!"

Behind the tall grass, there is a faded green sign, and this is what she is pointing at. *Now Entering Xania, Manitoba*, it says. *A 911 Community.* "Xania," she says in wonder. "This town. Xania."

Hal is laughing too now, his whole body heaving. "We need T-shirts. We need mugs. They must sell them somewhere." They both stare out the window, looking through the neck-high wheat which surrounds them. Xania passes by uneventfully—small, agricultural and devoid of souvenirs. It has a hardware store. It has a food store. It has a feed store. Nothing else, though, and it is quickly gone. But as they pass the *Now Leaving* sign and Hal stops the car to take a picture, they are still laughing. Titania knows that they will eventually stop laughing and that eventually the car will again be silent except for the grim march of the gravel beating against the back window, but right now there is laughter and motion and noise. She leans back in her seat. It is a happy moment, she thinks. It is also one which cannot last, a rare shared moment in a world which is slowly and inevitably forcing the two of them apart. But she does not dwell on these thoughts. After all, she's not the dwelling type.

Liam Young
The Day My Mother Phoned

Has this ever happened to you? Has someone ever called you on the telephone and asked if you'd eat food with them in the middle of the day? Has this ever happened? My mother loves restaurants and my mother loves lunch. I have never understood why restaurants exist or why people enjoy so much to eat surrounded by other people they don't know.

This is what happened to me: I had lunch with my mother.

My mother chose the place and I drove us there. It was a small Italian restaurant with high ceilings and dark yellow walls, and someone was playing the mandolin. On the walls hung paintings of Tuscan landscapes and in the corner there was a rubber plant that was bent and faded. It was twelve thirty and the place was filled with a lunch crowd of business executives dressed in fashionable suits. Like lab rats in a maze, they had been released from their cubicles and keyboards in order to search for food and water.

A waiter, dressed in black, greeted my mother and me with a nod of his head, and led us past the clamor of voices discussing interest rates and the stock exchange. We sat down at a table by the window and the waiter handed us leather-covered menus, and then he disappeared into the kitchen as we began scanning the food selection. I chose the only dish without meat, the pesto pasta. My mother could not decide.

She said to me, "Should I have the pasta and salad or the soup and salad?"

I said nothing. (I once believed this woman knew everything in the world that there was to know. Now she could not decide between soup or pasta without my assistance.)

"Well," she said, "soup or pasta?"

Again I said nothing and stared out the window. I saw an

131

Airedale pissing on a red fire hydrant. How classic, I thought, and just about laughed.

"Fine," she said to me. "If you're not going to speak, I'll just have to choose the soup; I'm not really that hungry anyway."

"Your shoes look nice," I said. I could tell they were new and that the purpose of this luncheon was to test out the new shoes. That's what happens when you get old: your life begins to shrink.

She said to me, "My shoes look nice? Do you realize that's the only thing you've said to me besides a grunt of a hello when you picked me up? Are you depressed? You can't even see my shoes, they're beneath the table!"

"I can remember," I said to her, and it was true, I could. They were small and black with a low heel and a pointed toe. "You're wearing them to match that black skirt and that white blouse."

The waiter returned with a basket of bread and asked if we were ready to order. My mother said, "No."

I tried to avoid talking with the waiter by looking out the window. That's when I saw him, the man in the coat. He walked past the window and entered the restaurant. He stood quivering by the entrance, and then he limped to the center of the dining room and stared at all the clean men and women. I buried my head in my menu and tried not to look at the only man standing in a room full of chairs. But my mother was not aware of the unspoken rule that you do not make eye contact with the mentally unstable. She squinted at him and twitched her nose. He walked over to our table. He had a pale sagging face and was wearing a gray trench coat that hung down to his bare ankles. On his feet he wore sandals. He was either half drunk or half sober, I couldn't tell which. But what I could tell was that this man was old and soon this man would be dirt. My mother's eyes widened and her lips curled back as she said to him, "Don't worry, things are good."

The man leaned over and said to my mother, "Why aren't you clapping for me, why aren't you clapping?"

Murray McCulloch
Country Snow

Here, gloves are no help at all.
The frost wears into the
ravines of my useless hands,
cold enough to burn.

Father sits in his den
reading from *Sorrows of Werther*,
while I clear a path to the stable.
His ponies have won shows across Europe,
their manes like chocolate.

Many winters passed this way,
him warm inside while I walk through the
rows of crystalline evergreens, tossing
salt. I used to dream of an ocean home

where my own children fed
and groomed the ponies while I sat
on the balcony watching the sunrise,
a pipe in the palm of my hand,
a leather bound bible resting open on my lap.

The lamp blinds me like the reflection
of sun on morning snow. I abandon my
shovel and salt and lean against the fence.
More flakes begin to drift down, erasing
years of work. An owl lands
on the branches above me, blocking the light.

Michael Mulley
The Window at Night

I cannot sleep
and the night seems a lifetime,
rest only a memory

like spelling bees and turtlenecks
archived in the back of my brain:
the amygdala, the medulla oblongata.

The Italian divas of anatomy,
won't leave their little rooms
unless I hammer on the windows.

Minutes ago, I was banging
on the plaster behind my pillow:
Tonight, I learned

we have a rat in our walls,
inches from my head,
scratching at the brick,

getting louder still: can the neighbors
hear? But through my window
I can see Neighbor Two

her face submerged
in the glow of an infomercial,
and now a tap, a blast

of trumpet and Neighbor Five
has begun to play his music and—

sigh, stomp, turn on the light.
The rat drums the brick

in tune with the rhythms
next door. A car honks. A Matisse
woman stares from the wall, the single fluid

stroke of her eyes and nose dancing
in time with music, rat, car,
all that jazz.

Ali Parker
Mainstream and Upstream

When I was thirteen they told me that I smelled like fish; those gum chewing girls, who shoplifted perfume and hair dye and always spoke loudly in class. They told me that. I thought about it for a bit and decided they were right. I pictured myself as a salmon. My scales flashing against the pebbly creek bottom as I boldly fought against the current. As a salmon it was my noble duty to spawn. I thrashed my tail with the desperate passion that only a salmon knows. My comrades dying left and right in dangerous shallows or under jagged rocks. I left them to stink, pink blood flowing in ribbons to the ocean, eyes filming over, finally at rest. I had to make it to the spawning grounds, that secret, sacred location. People don't know why we do it, fighting against the rapids, the shallows, but I know, why.

Janet Kwok
Losing My Chance With Paul H.

Friday in August, when I have time like pores on my face, I volunteer to cook dinner.

Good.

Bad: I shell all the shrimp into the garburator, where they were never intended to go. I even recall Mother quite vividly in a white halo-haze saying *Certain foods must NEVER enter The Garburator.* But something must have distracted me and I never learned about those Foods That Clog.

I shell a whole carton. My fingers are numb from plucking out the dozens of frosted nuggets, flicking them into the garburator. The trouble is there are no warning shots for me. No breaking of water. There is no blue smoke, harsh odor, dizziness or swelling.

Instead I go straight to the disease. First, water backs up. But water backing up is innocuous. After all, it returns clean and clear. Then, the sink begins to erupt shrimp bits. Sitting in front of the sink, all I hear is hiccuping—then vomiting in bursts. Mother quietly hardens from the influx of ocean odor and abnormal sounds; Father hauls up the Drāno. But the plumber has gone to Nova Scotia, so nothing matters till Saturday morning.

I know nothing about Drāno. I picture the dangerous, powerful substance which can dissolve *anything* as being teal, magenta or some shade of bridesmaid garb—terrifying and unnatural. But it is clear. Like vodka or water.

At first the water disappears down the drain.

Then the sound grows quieter and creeps back up to mock us.

Hu-u-u-u-h-h—a vein brews under Father's forehead. As he turns away, he appears to be drawing a knife from a scabbard but he merely scratches his pink neck. He flatly asks for the plunger and rolls up invisible sleeves.

Mother screams when she sees us lowering the plunger into the sink.

It's been in the toilet you idiots. It's been in feces. Now it's in our sink. With our food.

Father turns to her.

Mother leaves the kitchen and metes out rage upon my brother.

Bring three large buckets. Father nestles himself between large black pipes, garbage can and bottles of Sani-Foam in the bowels of the sink. He is sandwiched among pieces of stray waste and bits of food.

The shrimp are pumped into buckets. Shrimp are not the only treasures. There are bite-size pieces of lard and mysterious finger-sized lumps of ancient organic matter.

The blue translucent bucket darkens with sludge.

Go outside and dump it, okay?

But where? I imagine a silvery stream, a chunk-filled river crawling toward the adjoining neighborhood. The day care kids down the street will try to taste it; the toxic stream will pool at speed bumps.

No, in the sewer outside.

I am not even aware there is a sewer in front of the house. I walk down the stairs to the side door—the neighbor's kid is just in front. The door has frosted anti-shatter glass, so he is obscured, as if underwater. But which one? The youngest one? Or the romantically impossible one?

They are, after all, all behind glass.

It must be the oldest one. It's not a small blob. I creep closer to the window, knowing that he can probably see a fading and blooming pink splotch behind the glass. I press my back to the door. Should I keep my glasses on? My bangs are spiked from being pushed by my headband; my hair is twisted and forced upward like silk grass. The white blob shifts from side to side.

I squint at the memory of a dinner between our two families, months ago. Girls on one side, boys on the other—all flanked by parents. There is no feud preventing me from dropping by or calling, because feuds begin and someday end. But not the strings that we have been born into and automatically sense—sensing the way you know that sometimes, someone is watching you. These strings need no explanation, being so old they almost blend in—but what I do need explained is how he tried to talk to me at the dinner. Like a child's hand grazing the cookie jar on the high shelf.

I heave open the metal door.

It *is* him. He's locking up his bicycle.

Well, hi.

He is shocked out of embarrassment or shocked that I smell pickled. There is a flash where we both glance at each other at the same time. Did we always wear glasses?

We are alone, and I speculate upon a conversation in his pinned-open eyes.

What's in the bucket?

Sewage.

What kind of sewage?

There is only that twinkling—I have to keep walking, because I realize that nothing will happen. I hurry over in bare legs to the sewer. Have I shaved in the past six weeks? He didn't even say hi. In that fine blip, I did all the blinking.

Blindly, I hurl the bucket's cold slop out, splashing my bare dusty feet. I wonder if he has even gone in yet—or is he slyly watching me emptying sewage? I begin to aim the bucket more carefully, pouring more through the grating. When I turn, the bicycle isn't even leaning on the garage to prove I ever saw him. After I fling out the last clinging blobs, I watch my floating reflection, veiled by grating. He watched me flicker by: nervous, unpolished (unshaven), hunched over the sewer. He never saw the mercury-colored version: raised bangs quivering in the air, antennae intercepting signals.

Laura Ishiguro
yellow in a west coast virgin forest

that boneless color
ash and hollow stump seeping
with lichen; archipelago (how you slither
through the syllables)
that moult of bird yellow
sibilant
trails of slugs
the way my tongue moves
over my lips;
in my mouth
waiting to be born again and again

Adrienne Renton
How to Float

My family borrowed August, a month in a cabin
at Horn Lake, to tell us Annie was sick.

All night I dreamt, woke buried
in cotton sheets, sweat held Annie's hand.

"Bad dream?" she said. Dad was snoring,
Mom silent while we crept through the door.

Our feet padded over pebbles to the sand,
water yawning black as a cave.

I swear I saw monsters, glowing faces.
Annie told me they were stars.

I was afraid. I'd heard stories—water nymphs
twist around ankles with porcelain fingers,

squeeze children cold as December, with white fists
pull us to the lake bottom, tie us to black weeds.

My mother told us about chemotherapy, my father
showed us the weight of tears.

Annie didn't care, up to her waist in the lake,
water hiding half of her legs and hands.

"It's warm!" she called. I wanted to snatch her back
from mouths lined with teeth, back from eyes that never blink.

"It's warm out here!" she called again feet leaving bottom,
floating on the surface with the stars.

Boone Avasadanond
Rooster

Fallen champion,
your clean coat,
bleached white,
the angel that glowed
in the dim setting sun
chest flared,
the scream heard around the world:
this is my domain.
But like a drunk,
day and night to you
are now the same.

Once
you
made rivals
lose feathers
from their necks, their
eyes
staring anywhere other
than your direction.
You had your crowd:
here clucks the frenzied flock.
Everyone wants a piece of the champion.

Your feathers
stacked in a black bag
sit on the mud alongside
egg shells,
green chocolate wrappers, and
Lonny's wet diapers.

The dog rolls his loose old jaws,
your soft throat,
a dog bone,
a toothbrush.
Your guts
fed to the pigs,
your feet
sticking out of a Chinaman's mouth.
On my birthday
you chill in the oven,
and watch
without a head
from my mother's kitchen,
the honored seat.

Justine Durrant
Orbit

In the photograph
a mother holds her baby girl
toward a birthday cake.
Dad anticipates the wish
trapped in curls
of candle smoke.

I remember candles,
learning to run
my finger through the flame
again and again
black but not burnt.

It is a simple matter this wish business
the night sky forcing you to realize
what's important,
what's really on your mind,
not enough stars
for all these wishes.

I needed a meteor shower,
got a plane, a 747
blinking red and blue
Flight #27A, New York to Milan
or maybe it was a satellite
in orbit.

These days the stars fall
out of the sky
into my hand, a fist
glowing from the inside.

In the photograph
the baby girl learns to wish
while her parents, who have practiced
for years,
search the sky for stars.

I want to see that baby
recognize herself in a mirror
for the first time,
reach out to her own hand
and know the world
is round.

Jess Auerbach
The Skipping Song

Oh yes dem children dey happy-happy
dey roll dat box-cart down hill lucky-lucky
an sing oh Jesus da savior ahm saved
and jump in da box-cart down wid a smell of lemonade

fathers in the she-been
mama's with the madam
gogo cannot feed us all
the puppy's name is Tannin

Oh dem children dey go to da river
an der bodies aint flubby so dey got to shiver-shiver
dey singin, dey shoutin, dey jugglin wid some castle cans
dey don' look at da factory so's not to see da blood-bands

fathers in the she-been
mama's with the madam
gogo had to feed us all
the puppy's name was Tannin

Oh dem children dey got to learn at school
bein all domkop jus ain't really cool
but dey don' learn nothing wid a gun for a pen
an da box-cart might break before standard ten

fathers in the she-been
mama is a maid
gogo passed on yesterday
mama wasn't paid

Oh yes dem children dey happy-happy
dey roll dat box-cart down the hill lucky-lucky
an sing oh Jesus da savior ahm saved
an jump in da coffin wid a smell of lemonade

Jeremy Hanson-Finger
The Prime Mover

God expands nine percent upon freezing.
God costs two-tenths of a cent per gallon
in the continental United States.
An acre of corn contributes more
to the percentage of God in the atmosphere
than a lake of the same size.
One part gasoline can contaminate a mixture of
approximately seven hundred and fifty thousand parts God.
In twenty-one years, one in three people could be threatened by
an absence of God.
Nicotine God for smokers could hook kids, a watchdog reports.
Blacks in Detroit do not believe in privatizing God.
Each day the sun evaporates one trillion tons of God, but
the amount of God has remained the same for two billion years.
Three thousand four hundred cubic miles of God
are locked within the bodies of living things:

the human body is two-thirds God,
but a tree is three-quarters.

Brendan Inglis
The Uselessness of Spain

When does one need Spain?
So far in my life I have never
ever
ever
needed Spain, or Czechoslovakia.
I could manage fine without Spain,
even Europe, for that matter.
What is the use of any country?
All of Asia so far has aided me only slightly,
although many things are produced there, I hear.
And the Middle East has oil,
but, the truth is, most people think
they would be better off without
the turmoil and war.
I have to say Africa is pretty useless too, and everybody knows
Antarctica is just a waste of space
Australia is just good for the comical accents.
JFK said it best:
it's not what your country can do for you
because, really,
when you think about it
they don't know much.

Emma Kennedy
Dumb Fish Dying Near A Cabin At Dawn

It was a summer that shone like chalk.
Nothing would float but dead fish.
They looked the way old cheese smells,
the kind you buy at The Pinantan General Store,
the kind Uncle Craig would buy.
We slept in the bunk beds 24/7,
on the porch,
in the ferns.
We decided cabins are way too cold for internal heating.
I called Carol, the editing guru, today. She said the story needs a
purpose.
The slippery ants of creativity, insanity, and pretentiousness
crawled up the walls of my body.
They climbed like flames,
smelled like charcoal,
tasted like ink on recycled paper.
Extroverted hermits in claustrophobic fields,
they slipped into trees and walked around in them,
touching the bark from inside where it's softer.
But Emmalina couldn't get inside.
She will one day,
when tired of the scientific nostalgia that
surrounds her head with plaintive universes
and moaning song lyrics.
You can't understand a song until before you've heard it.
"Nous ne comprenons pas, nous sommes les idiots,"
say the sky, the cabin, the fish.
They floated silently,
dying in cold water under the chalk-flaking summer sun.

Samantha Wilde
Thin Ice

My father holds me up while we skate.
Me, tiny, grinning
as we face the camera.
My red toque matches my snowsuit,
my dad's face lined with fur, hat bulging out;
head like an eggplant,
black like his pants, his skates spread apart on the ice.
The clouds, almost pink,
make the snow around the frozen pond
glitter in shadows at its edges, the rushes
brave enough to poke their yellows and browns through the snow.
You can't see my mum behind the lens,
or the farm house up the hill to your right
its gray wood revealed by years of
prairie winters, scorching summers.
My father looks up smiling, doesn't notice beneath the hem of
          my snow pants
my bare ankle glowing above my skate:
a small stripe of red.
Perhaps I have fallen,
skid marks show blue-green ice,
at three, not yet having mastered the art
of balancing on sharp steel,
not yet afraid
of venturing onto thin ice.

Shannon Corregan
Friday Nights in Quidi Vidi

I didn't think, when I first came to Newfoundland, that there'd
be turquoise water anywhere around The Rock, but here we
are in Quidi Vidi Gut, and the water, while cold, is a remark-
ably clear pea-green. Or at least it would be, if it wasn't one in
the morning. This is how Wish and I spend our Friday nights.
We don't go to bars, we don't vandalize street signs and we
don't cruise around St. John's in Civics that won't make it over
the speed bumps; we load a pack with beer and set our kayaks
in the Gut.

The Gut's nothing special, just a small cove with greasy
shore-side docks, rusty fishing boats and dories with motors
hitched up to the butt (stern, technically, but dories are small
enough that nautical terms don't apply). It's protected from the
Atlantic by a natural, craggy-looking rock face. A few centuries
ago, some genius fishermen built stilt houses along the rock,
and now they're heritage sights. They interfere with the passage
of bigger ships, because the Gut's a tight squeeze and trollers
have to be extra careful not to smack the houses with their
stabilizers.

You know, anyone else would have called it Quidi Vidi Cove,
just for the alliteration, but not the Newfoundlanders.

Some people say kayaking's therapeutic. They are wrong.
While kayaking with Allouiscious (he prefers Wish) isn't
physically taxing, there's no way in hell you can call it relaxing.
By the time we're out of Quidi Vidi, we're arguing. It's the
weekly ritual. Some guys play soccer, some guys play cards,
we argue.

Tonight, we start with God, and take off from there. It begins
even before we push off the gravel boat launch. It continues
through the harbor, through the tarred piers, out the rock pass,

into the open sea, where the water's choppy, even in late spring. There we pause for breath and beer. It's a moonless night, and the earth happens to be round, so we couldn't have seen it anyway, but directly across the water is Ireland.

Once lubricated, we set our paddles in the waves; Wish takes a deep breath, and he's off. "You're wrong, you know."

I pull my duct-taped paddle out of the water mid-stroke and smack Wish's fiberglass shell. "It's subjective, you blowhard! How the hell am I wrong if it's a matter of opinion?"

"Perhaps because your argument sucks."

"Please explain to me, my conceited redneck, how my argument sucks."

"Because black holes aren't matter—they're nothing, they're zero. If God made the universe, then He created black holes. Anything divided by zero is one, just as infinity divided by zero is one. God is infinite; one is not infinity; God has negated Himself."

The thing about Wish is, you can't really tell if he's plastered or not, because he talks like an encyclopedia all the time. He could be dying of alcohol poisoning, and no one would ever know until he keeled over mid-sentence. In fact the only way to tell if Wish has been at the bottle—and this is only if you have a good ear—is that his accent gets a wee bit more Newfoundlandish. (The Newfoundland accent, by the by, is harsh, metallic and basically just an inclination to abuse long vowels and treat *th* and *d* like *t*.) Wish told me my inability to argue has very little to do with my idiocy and more to do with my low alcohol tolerance, which isn't fair at all, because I hold my liquor pretty well. It's just that Wish is a Newfoundlander. Wish can out-drink anybody except his dad, his uncle and the Irish.

"Ah, but by saying that, you imply that there previously was a God, and so you're accepting that He must have existed once." People are more severely God-fearing on this side of the country, the good old clay-o'-the-earth types, so it's funny that I'm religious and Wish isn't. Wish disbelieves in God so strongly, and can argue so well when drinking, that even old So-krates would have a hard time disproving him.

"No, I merely stated that God could not exist. However, since you replied to my argument, you acknowledged its legitimacy. And as a believer, by accepting my negation of Him, you've successfully negated yourself and therefore your argument. I win."

"Listen, if God is infinite, then he created black holes. Black holes mean zero, and anything divided by zero is one. God is infinite, and so is the universe, and infinity divided by infinity is one. The universe is reduced to One God."

"Congratulations. You have just proven God's existence through mathematics." He splashes me with a flick of his paddle. To be sure, this reaction is an improvement on last time. The last time I proved the existence of God through math, we were on land, and he threw me out the front door and locked it behind me. He refused to open it until I had apologized for offending the sensibility of the universe. I had to climb up the woodpile onto the roof of the shed so I could knock on his mother's window and convince her to let me back in.

It's late now; we head back to the Gut. I can't see the lights of the harbor anymore, but I'm not worried. Wish has the migratory sense of a homing pigeon. We're arguing again, this time about beer. By the time we're home safe in the Gut, we're throwing the empties at each other. Our Friday nights usually end with us throwing things, or playing chicken, or swordfighting with the paddles, which is why mine is held together with tape. When we're injured and exhausted, we abandon our violent drunkenness and resign ourselves to more passive drunkenness. We bob between the dinghies, drink our beer and argue about our previous argument. I usually start, because I'm usually the one with the wounded pride. Tonight, for once, Wish begins the bitching.

"My argument was flawless!" he maintains. "It just failed on a technicality."

"Ah-hah! You admit that it failed, then?"

"Merely on a technicality."

"So it was, technically, a failure?"

"Yzbah!"

He does this a lot, the bastard. I'm unfamiliar enough with Newfoundlandese that I can't tell whether he's talking slang or talking nonsense. I have three beers in me and my ears are humming; I assume I haven't heard him right. "Huh?"

"Mwa-bah-hah!" He throws his head back in his best evil laugh. "I win! Any single-syllable argument that is followed by a statement with a ridiculous number of syllables, such as this one, becomes an infinitesimal fraction when you divide them, and (as proven by mathematicians trying to take the sum of the infinite series) becomes so small that it isn't recognizable as a viable, workable number. Your argument is now so small that it no longer exists. Therefore, you had nothing to say in response to my previous argument, so you let my last point go by unchallenged; silence is as good as agreement, and therefore you are defeated."

"Wish, I don't tell you this enough, but you suck."

"Mwa-hah-hah!" Wish hands me the beer and disengages himself from his kayak. He slides into the waist-deep water as dexterously as a sober man.

"Christ, that's cold!"

"Hey, if you don't believe in Christianity, then you don't get to swear like a Christian. Besides, it's not that cold."

With a pained sigh, like I don't know what's good for me, he reaches out to grab the side of my kayak. It's usually tricky to tip a kayak, but these are cheapos, and I've got nothing on Wish as far as biceps are concerned. The black plane of water swings up, hits me in the side of the head, and suddenly I'm under. The night's warm—it's summer, after all—but this is still the Atlantic, boys and girls. Fortunately, I'm also a bit sloshed, so the temperature doesn't bother me much. I'm not nervous—I've rolled a kayak before—but the primal part of my brain is insistently reminding me that there's no air underwater. I've got no momentum left; I can't roll back up. After a few tries, my common sense kicks in, and I begin to negotiate my way out of the kayak. The skirt gets in my way—so do my limbs, and I smack my head on something—but eventually Wish takes pity on me and helps me to my feet.

"I stand corrected; it's goddamn freezing."

Wish hands me my paddle and we slosh up to the boat launch, tugging our waterlogged kayaks behind us. "You know, if you handled your alcohol with a little more grace, this wouldn't be a problem. Where's the beer?"

We halt, knee-deep now, and turn to stare out over the black water of the Gut. There's no hope of finding anything there that isn't phosphorescent.

"It was a sign," he says reverently, patting me on the back. "From God. You lost the beer. A sure sign of your inferiority. My argument was the righteous winner. Anyways, it's all for the best. The apple in the Garden of Eden was alcohol."

"Actually, it was knowledge. Besides, wine's the blood of Christ, or something like that. He flows through us and makes us stronger."

"And stupider."

"I don't think that's a word. You know, if you didn't outweigh me by thirty pounds, and if your mother didn't feed me every night, I would seriously think about kicking your ass. Let's go, I'm freezing."

We haul our kayaks up the gravel slope. He doesn't have racks, so we tie them onto the roof of his Volvo—brown, rusty and beaten in true Newfoundland fashion.

Claire Mackenzie
Climbing the Water Tower

Fat black Spider crawls across my hand, mistakes me for cement.
I understand. I feel like a part of this harsh gray place. My hair
and skin look washed out in this hard light. Spider scuttles
under a blackberry branch, finds safety in a cluster of berries
that are rotting in the brutal sun. I watch, lose track of him in
the spiky undergrowth.

*I'm seven years old. Adrienne tosses her reddish brown curls
over her shoulder, tells me she loves my hair, wishes she had straight
blond hair like mine. She asks me if she can cut it to look like the
model in the magazine. Takes out her safety scissors.*

Adrienne attracts my eye; she looks vivacious as usual,
turning cartwheels with Jen on the concrete beneath the old
water tower. Adrienne's scarlet tank top flips up, shows tanned
skin that stands out clearly against the drab background of
brambles, rock and rusted steel. I hate it here, even Jen would
rather be at the beach, but Adrienne is here. Where she leads,
Jen follows, and I, like the good little lap dog, follow them both.

*I'm eleven years old. At a party, Adrienne dares me to kiss Tyler
Wilson, the boy who sits in front of me at school. Her mother bursts
in with snacks; Adrienne giggles.*

Adrienne is already bored with cartwheels; she rarely
concentrates on anything for long. Her gaze sweeps the area,
lights on the water tower. "Let's climb the water tower."

My heart stops. I look up, my gaze follows the ladder to
where a thin platform circles the tower. It is breathtakingly
high up. I feel a sense of utter inevitability as I take in all the
rust and decay on the fragile old ladder. It hasn't been used in
how many years, three, five, ten? Fear rolls in the pit of my
stomach. Adrienne has taken charge; there will be no turning
back now.

I'm thirteen years old. Adrienne tells me she misses me, we haven't hung out in ages. She tells me I should join soccer, we would have practices together twice a week. I sign up. Adrienne gets her first real boyfriend, has to cut back on her after-school activities to make time for him.

Jen goes first. She had been in gymnastics since she was a toddler. She stops halfway, gives a little whimper, keeps going. Cheers when she reaches the top, basking in Adrienne's shouted approval. It's too high for me to see her face.

I'm fifteen years old. We have gone to the midnight showing of a movie with some friends. I'm supposed to be getting a ride home with Adrienne. Adrienne has a new boyfriend and has been rather forgetful lately.

Adrienne looks at me expectantly. I look up again, at the tiny doll-like figure that is Jen waving at us. I picture the ladder breaking, the impact of my body on the cement, crushing the blackberries. I shake my head. "I...I can't," I falter. Adrienne hugs me, encouraging me in a soothing voice.

"You can do it," and "I believe in you." Right now there is nothing I want more than to be able to make Adrienne smile at me in the approving way she smiled at Jen. I shake my head again, because not even sunny, laughing Adrienne can make me brave the tower. Adrienne shrugs, removes the sweater wrapped around her waist and turns to the ladder. I wait behind, misery a tangible hand on my shoulder.

I'm seventeen years old. Adrienne cannot convince me to climb the rusty old water tower. I wait on the cement at the bottom. Adrienne and Jen come back down, laughing and ignoring me. Fat black Spider crawls across Adrienne's sweater, mistaking it for cement. Adrienne shrieks and jumps back, yells, "Kill it! Kill it!" Jen runs about, hides behind Adrienne. I tip Spider off the sweater. He scuttles under a blackberry branch, finds safety in a cluster of berries that are rotting in the brutal sun. I feel brave again.

159

Sarah Obee
Adelante

You are high on the Christmas scent of oranges, your thumb-nail is yellow with their skin. You sit on the chesterfield with your bare feet on the coffee table. Nearby, he runs the vacuum cleaner in his hands. You wonder how he keeps his nails so clean. He eats as many oranges as you do.

Tonight you will have guests. "They'll understand," you say, meaning if the house is not clean. You are high on the scent of oranges. You want him. You want a hand cupping your breast, clean fingernails skimming your spine.

"They'll be here soon," he says. The vacuum whirs. Pine needles clink inside the tube.

"I know," you say. You like the risk. When he passes with the vacuum, you wrap your blue-jeaned legs around his until he kisses you. You'd write a book about the sugarplum taste of his lips if you were any good at spelling.

Soon his family arrives. His parents speak Spanish when they don't want you to know what they're saying. They do not approve of you, of your living arrangement. You do your best to please them. You fold your hands delicately in your lap and ask if anyone would like an orange. "No," they say. Afterward, your boyfriend will tell you that you should just be yourself, but you don't feel comfortable. With his brothers, it's different. They don't care. You push their Hotwheels race cars around the bathroom floor, crash them against the bathtub, marvel as they change color in cold water.

You show his mother around the apartment. The kitchen, where he's cooking supper, reading and re-reading the cookbook instructions. The living room, with a neatly vacuumed carpet but footprints on the coffee table. The workroom with your desk, lost beneath a swarm of papers, and his desk, organized. The bedroom that you share. On his side, everything is picked off the floor, hidden neatly away. On your side is the television, clothes flung over a chair, books you haven't had the time to read. Post-It notes, orange peels. You grow embarrassed, dart around the room, scoop the litter into the garbage can. You tell his mother you've been too busy studying to clean. She gives you a knowing smile. You don't know if it's okay to relax. You tear the tube of deodorant from the top of the television and toss it into a dresser drawer. Maybe she didn't notice.

Your parents leave messages on the answering machine. You write them all down on Post-It notes whose backs have lost their stick. They think you should work harder in your classes. They think you should go to university closer to home. Your older brother thinks you're not ready to live with your boyfriend. He once insulted you and hung up. You copied it down in your neat handwriting: *Whore.* It fell off the refrigerator the next day. You lost it among the certificates your teachers give you at fancy evening ceremonies. You do not believe you deserve all these awards, all this calligraphy. They're all for "effort" anyway. You throw the certificates into your room and forget about them. Your desktop is a confetti mess, so you use your boyfriend's for scribbling homework. He doesn't mind, says he loves the way your thumb, with its yellow nail, bends to and fro as you dart big words across the margins. Your major is Greek and Roman Studies. His is Music Education. You'll never get jobs, either of you. Together you'll live in poverty, waxing Euripides and waning Vivaldi. He minors in Spanish Literature. Sometimes he reads you Cervantes, Neruda, in his native tongue. You took Spanish in high school. All you remember is "adelante." "Forward." You say that's what you want to name your daughter. He says maybe that's a bit forward. He adds, "Get it? Forward?" You don't laugh.

Your boyfriend hates that you screen your calls. He wishes you would talk to your parents. You tell him that being a goody-goody never got anybody anywhere. It's a line you heard on TV. He knows you don't believe it.

Later, when you're picking through the papers strewn all over your desk, searching for your notes on Ovid, he enters with the cordless phone in hand. It's for you. It's your mother. She asks about school. You tell her it's fine, thank her tersely for paying half your tuition fees. She asks about your apartment. You pretend you're not standing on a pile of unwashed T-shirts as you promise to send photos of your lovely abode. Then you wave your eavesdropping boyfriend out of the room. Your mother tells you of a magazine article she read. "Unmarried couples who live together are less likely to stay together." You tell her of a magazine article you read. "Women who stay single enjoy better mental health than those who marry." She accuses you of not listening to her. You ask to speak to your father.

He's quiet for a moment before he asks if you're pregnant. You're not sure what he really means. "Of course not," you quickly reply, and then you tell him you've been eating a lot of oranges lately, getting lots of Vitamin C. He likes to hear you're healthy. Both your parents say they miss having you at home. They wish you had come home for Christmas. You tell them your next school break isn't until March, remind them how much you hate to fly.

After the phone call, your boyfriend asks if there was an argument. You realize there wasn't one, not out loud, but you feel guilty as if you had just splintered all of your father's old Beatles records, spilt wine on your mother's dresses. You can't let your boyfriend know this. You smile, laugh a little, tell him you just have to get used to being apart from your parents. After all, you reason, someday they'll die, and then you'll have to be apart from them for the rest of your life. This thought makes you feel worse, sick. You go to the kitchen and rip all the Post-Its from the fridge. They sit on the floor overnight. When you try to put them back, they refuse. When they fall, they form a pile on the floor like leaves in hot pink, neon green, ugly magenta.

Your boyfriend had braces in elementary school, but they've long been off and now his teeth sit in his mouth like thirty-two rectangular moons. He plans dentist appointments into his daily life, says having his teeth cleaned is like a massage for his gums. He tells you that when he was younger, he wanted to be an orthodontist, wanted perhaps to woo and marry the tooth fairy. You clamp your mouth shut in response. You're no tooth fairy. You go to the dentist every six months just so the secretary will stop phoning you. X-rays show cracks in your brushing technique. You pretend to gag easily so they feel bad about poking their spiked tools into your molars. The final check brings nothing but lectures. "Buckle on one-seventeen." You think of a shoe buckle. The dentist code is bogus.

Your birthday is in April. Your boyfriend brings you a child's toy, a plastic crocodile with removable teeth. A joke gift. A joke gift with the price tag still on. This is what your eighteenth birthday is worth to him. You sit on the kitchen floor, playing dentist to a reptile. It whirs across the linoleum, its jaws crunch up and down. You run your tongue along your jagged incisors and wonder what it's like to kiss you, what it's like to kiss a crocodile, a monster with no teeth.

One Saturday, you set out to shop for groceries, but you never make it to the store. An idea strikes you while you're passing the bus stop. You're reminded of something you've always wanted to do. When the next bus pulls to a stop you don't even ask its destination before hopping aboard. You want to ride the bus the whole day, changing directions whenever you please. You want to see where you'll end up, what new people you'll meet.

By one o'clock you're bored and tired and force yourself to step off. You don't know where you are. You call your boyfriend to beg for a ride home. He tells you you're usually smarter than that, but rushes to find you. Together you do the grocery shopping. Milk, bread, peanut butter, two boxes of Mandarin oranges. He has to pay for it. You used all your change on the buses. You'd get a bank account if you were any good at saving money.

You're good at saving poppies. All through November you walk with your eyes on the floor of your university's stretching hallways. You watch the bare patches of sidewalk, the sparkling patches of snow, all in the hope of finding a fake red flower you can pin to the bottom of your bedroom curtains. The current count is thirteen. Six on one side, seven on the other. This makes you nervous. It's uneven, it's unlucky. Now it's December and you're desperate. You tell your boyfriend to be on the lookout too. You tell him the thirteen poppies will throw your love life into turmoil. He asks why you can't just take away one poppy to have twelve. You know he thinks poppies are depressing anyway. He finds photos of headstones with poppies sleeping at their feet. Someone's mother could be buried there, he says. Someone's father. You ignore him, threaten to start biting your nails again unless this problem is resolved. He tells you you're immature. You think he wants to say "annoying." You stop talking about your thirteen poppies.

When you're depressed, you lie on the roof and let it sink in. When he comes in search of you, you begin to plead. You want to tell him he shouldn't love you, you haven't done anything to deserve it, but you know he'd make you take it back. He wraps himself around you like an orange peel, whispers ten things he loves about you. The green flecks in your eyes, the sandals you'll wear until the first snowfall, the way you cry at Tim Horton's commercials. The next night, you find him lying on the sweet pea-yellow bedspread with a photo album rising and falling on his chest. "Merry Christmas," he whispers with a shy smile. The album is a collage. "A year in certificates, in phone message Post-It notes," he calls it. It's hard to believe you've lived together that long, but you're glad you have.

Now you can use your desk again. You sneak away and write a list. Nine things you love about him. The way he wears a winter coat until July, the way he makes you laugh when you're panicking, his black hair. You fumble on the tenth. The way he never gives up on you is what you finally write, and you return to the bedroom to tell him. He squeezes your hand, falls asleep in your arms like a baby, the baby you will name Adelante.

You're folding dishtowels
at three in the morning,
pressing the linen's sharp
creases to the rhythm of
some campfire song
you haven't heard in years.
It's stuck in your mind like
a penny in tar.

You've tried everything.

Counting sheep
disturbs you,
wooly masses hurtling
over your bed.
You cannot picture them
landing safely on their
wobbly hoofs.

You name countries
alphabetically.
        Albania.
        Bulgaria.
        Cambodia.
        Denmark.

In the ravaged quiet
you notice things:
rain charging
from gutters.

Ethiopia.
The way darkness pulls
at the road.
Finland.
You think about
the insides of your eyelids,
conscious of their pinkness,
the way they flutter
with the passing of cars.

You catch
yourself smoothing
you hair
with your fingers.

You've thought
all the way to
Zambia
but there is no country
as far away as sleep.

Shannon Corregan
The Pirate Monologues, Nice, Room 305

in Nice, our room was small and lemon-scented
the curtains, cheap, thin,
snapped taut on an accordion breeze
street musicians played drinking tunes
in the outside square where
from 1789 to 1799
skulls bounced and rolled into gutters

in daylight we were dinghies
tied to our teacher-guides by halyards
we floated through the tours like ghosts
past wattle and daub and Renaissance walls
past scalloped Roman columns
and temples dedicated to Poseidon
past Medieval castles where ferns
virgin green
unfurled their spores through cracks like sails
to catch the lift of winter sun

we walked up stairs worn clean
from centuries of prisoners' feet
our adolescent hands followed the rigging
of Greek sailing ships
painted in blood on prison-tower walls
we trailed our palms over the rust stains
where manacles hung
in the evening
we pressed our ears
against the door to room 306
listening for our chaperone's heavy breathing

You watched a storm come from over the canyon
with your daughter.
Do you remember how she clung to you tightly
from the back of the bike
as you tried to outride the thunder?

Robyn Plasterer
Two White Wings

*"All the great things are simple and many can be expressed
in a single word: freedom."*
WINSTON CHURCHILL

Newton got it wrong.
Every object in a state of uniform motion
longs for release.

Even the mountains ache for sky
reach out from mother Gaea
breathe autonomy
against the bracing wind.

Maslow told us of our need to belong.
Did he forget our need to break free?

The egg came first
to teach us emancipation.
We are all chickens
layer upon layer of evolution
attempting to escape.

Picasso tried to capture it
true irony
the one thing which refuses to be caught.

It's not about chains
and it's not about speech.
We all know it's bigger than that.

It wears a simple loincloth
and sits at a spinning wheel
waiting to march to the Arabian Sea.

We give it names like
Malcolm, Mandela.
Names that pulsate in our mouths.

It can be drowned and broken
or burned in Auschwitz.
But it is victorious
without ever knowing victory.

And it does not fly in any flag.
It's not a torch over New York.
Not even the words in this poem.

It is a fluid.
A distant tide
that rolls through us like waves
away from every shore.

It is not about the dove,
or any single life.
It is the living air,
the silent beating of two white wings.

Leanna Wong
Learning Our Language

At the Chinese Public School, Grade One
I played this game for the first time.
You told me this was how in China students learned to read.
You called it in English (with a Cantonese zing)
Spelw Back
I imagined the straight backs of school uniforms,
Chinese characters marched up spinal cords.

In a sea of thousands of characters I only knew a few.
You said trace them on my back.
I smoothed the wrinkles with the flat of my small hand.
My finger, a hollow stick of bamboo stuffed with goat's hair,
        dipped in ink.
On your rice paper T-shirt,
scrawled the first character that came to mind: *I*

You unraveled my left hand like a scroll
the thick stub of your index finger,
stiff strokes etched into my palm.
In your fluent tongue you chanted
the order of strokes.

Like a mantra I repeated in my mind
top to bottom, left to right
chose the next character to draw,
my finger posed with confidence until you turned
in my direction,
took my hand, corrected me again:
Dis is how you spelw "Love"

You counted the strokes out loud:
yat, yee, saam...
Like a dance on my palm.
Stopped on ten.
Told me I forgot to add the second dot on the heart.

I wiped the creases on your shirt.
My brain mulled over length, curve and position of each line.
I brushed in slow, solid strokes
and drew the final tick with a quick sweep of goat hair.
I could see the faint inscriptions in the rice paper,
it read:
Father.
You reached for my hand,
dotted the heart of my palm with your lips.

Danielle Hubbard
Abduction

Andy stood beside me with his hand on the fence. His nose was sunburned.

He said, "What're you looking at, Hannah?"

"The telescope." I pointed up to the house: the second floor window. That was the window of our bedroom, my brother Andy's and mine. The telescope was just visible, like one eye watching. "Why aren't we bringing it?" I said.

"I don't want to. You can get it if you care."

I looked away from the house. "I don't want to leave."

"I think we have to." He was ten. I was eight. He stuck his hands in his pockets, walked back across the lawn, past the herb garden without looking at it, didn't wobble along the stepping stones. He went around the corner of the house and out of sight. If I listened, I'd be able to hear the foster workers' voices. But I knew I'd be hearing them soon enough. Hostile species, I thought. Commander, they could be dangerous. Commander?

I rested my chin on my arms and looked out over the fields: the wheat of Deep Space. My hand stung where I'd cut it. I didn't want to leave.

Andy and I slept in the same room. He had the upper bunk, and I had the lower. That way, said Mom, we couldn't see each other undress or anything. It wouldn't be perverted. She said that when I was five, the summer before she left.

That summer she took us to church every Sunday, though Daddy never came along. She wore a feathered hat, sort of crooked so it shaded her face. Andy and I would sit on either side and try to whisper plans across her lap. She always caught us

and she would smile—the Sunday smile that came with lipstick—
and hold our wrists as we listened to the sermon. Some days
she forgot to take off her hat. On other days she remembered.
On the best days, she let me try it on.

After the service, Mom never hurried to leave. She would
stay around and fold tablecloths with the pastor's wife. The
other kids all left, and Andy and I would sit on the front steps
and draw aliens in the dust with our fingers. I always offered to
help with the tablecloths, like sometimes I did at home, but at
church Mom had a special laugh, and a special smile, and she
never wanted my help.

The telescope was stationed by Andy's headboard, in the
alcove of the window. It looked out over the herb garden—the
asteroid belt—over the lawn, and then away into Deep Space.
When it was dark, Andy would smuggle in a flashlight and shine
it down the ladder so I could climb—enough light to see by, not
enough for Daddy to notice. Once I was up, we turned off the
torch, and the stars came out as bright as Christmas lights.

We had a hobby of watching for UFOs.

"You know, Hannah," said Andy. It was night and we sat
together by the window. "Aliens aren't really green."

"What do you mean?"

"I mean, they're not necessarily green. They might be
yellow." He shrugged. "I mean, yellow for instance."

"Pink?"

"Naw. Pink is girly."

"I saw one once that was pink," I said. "It came in a really
little spaceship." I cupped my hand. "Only that big. It was really
little."

"I bet you're lying."

"No, it was by the fence."

"When?"

"Yesterday." My face against the window, I pointed out into
the dark. "It was there, by the broken board where the rabbits

get through. And the pilot—he was little too—he asked me the way to the spaceport, and I told him that we didn't have one yet, because Daddy wouldn't give us the change to buy a box or anything for the landing pad, but that we were saving up, so if he came back tomorrow…" I caught Andy's look, the way he raises one eyebrow when he doesn't believe me. "Okay, day after tomorrow. I told him that if he came back the day after tomorrow, we'd probably have somewhere he could land."

"You're lying," said Andy.

"No, I'm not. I swear. You can put it in the Log, 'cause I *did* see it."

"*You* put it in the Log."

I pushed away from the window and folded my arms. That was how Andy got his power; he could write and I couldn't. It made him the master of the Log, where we recorded all the ships we'd seen, all the extra-terrestrials we'd talked to. It was a great feat when one of my discoveries made it in. Mostly Andy didn't believe me. He believed himself a lot, though. He had communication links with the ships from all over the place: Orion, Sagittarius and even a colony of jellyfish aliens that lived in the middle of a star called "Andy's Sun." I said, wasn't that a little mean of him to name a whole sun after himself? But he said that no, it wasn't, because no one had thought to name it before, not even the jellyfish, and that it wasn't fair to not have a name.

Andy crawled through the blankets to the backboard, where he reached beneath the mattress and pulled out the Log. It was a notebook that Daddy had bought me for school— forgot that I was in grade one and couldn't write yet—so I'd smuggled it home again, and now it was the Log instead. Andy opened it and flipped to the last entry. He turned on the flashlight and held it crooked in his armpit.

"You see the light there?" He pointed. A yellow dot, like a firefly, pulsed in the distance. "I bet it's a spy ship from Galtron."

"Really?"

"Looks like it." Andy began to write, and that was the cue to shut up. He mouthed the words as he wrote them and stopped at the end of each sentence to sharpen his pencil.

Around the front of the house came the sound of tires over gravel. Andy's hand stopped. Daddy was home. The front door swung, and a radio switched on. The door slammed.

"Hah, bitch!" It was Daddy's voice up the stairwell. Cupboard doors crashed—open, closed. "Why haven't you gone shopping? No food in the house. What is this shit? Here's the porcelain the pastor gave us, huh?" Something smashed on the floor. "What's a pastor doing giving people china? I'll sell it to the thrift shop next. Buy some food for your kids. Jesus! You leave me with the brats, you..."

Andy wrapped his arms around my head. It was meant to be my shoulders, but really he got my head. "You better get down," he said. He meant to my own bunk, and I nodded into his chest. He always smelled like chickens, but I didn't mind, and I would have stayed with him all night if he'd let me. I hate it when Daddy talks to himself.

The next day was Monday, though I didn't know it. Every day was the same: chores. Except when Daddy forgot and went to the fields without giving us any. In the summer it's hard to keep track of the days; there's no school, and no Mom in her feathered hat, feathered purse, to take us to church on Sundays. But the next day *was* Monday, and Andy was awake and already in the kitchen when I came down.

He leaned against the counter, eating an apple.

"Be careful, Hannah." Beside the window, bits of porcelain covered the floor: shiny white, edged in flowers. The cupboard over the stove was empty.

I stepped around the pieces and pointed at his apple. "Is it ripe?"

"Does it look ripe?"

"I don't know."

"Of course not," he said. "Look how tiny it is. They won't be ripe until October."

"Where's Daddy?" I said.

"On the front porch. He's asleep."

"Oh." I took a carton of milk and a box of cereal from the fridge; we kept the cereal there so it was easier to find. I poured myself a bowl and took a crusted orange spoon from the sink.

"That's gross, you know." Andy bit his apple. "Eat quick. There's gonna be a storm. The clouds are crazy." He swallowed. "A whole bunch of UFOs could be hiding in them."

I stuffed the spoon in my mouth and glared. It tasted of tomato soup.

"You look like a gopher," said Andy.

I tried to say something back but sprayed flakes across the table. I shut my mouth.

"Okay, good enough." He pulled my arm. "You're done, okay?"

"No!"

"But we have to get to the telescope! Man the defenses!" When I still didn't move, he said, "We're gonna be invaded. You can finish your cereal later."

"It'll go mushy," I said, but I stood up all the same and followed him up the stairs and up the ladder to the top bunk. Over Deep Space, clouds gathered like potatoes: the mashed ones that Mom had made with gravy and pepper that tasted like dirt.

It was what she made the last day. We didn't know it was the last one. She made gravy because the pastor was coming, and his wife, for dinner. We ate in the dining room. Mom had cleaned it all day and wouldn't let me help. Andy and I sat at the end of the table and made pyramids with the green beans on our plates. Daddy was quiet all through dinner and kept looking at the clock.

After dinner there was pie. Mom baked it in the morning and burnt the top crust. I found her crying as she scraped it off. But the pastor didn't know and he said it was good. While the rest of us were eating, Mom went upstairs to powder her nose, and the pastor went upstairs a few minutes later without giving an explanation. That left Daddy and the pastor's wife, but they had nothing to say to each other.

When Daddy finished his pie, he looked at the clock. He went upstairs and started shouting and stamped above our heads until our pyramids fell down, and Andy held my hand underneath the table.

Mom came down with her feathered purse. She had her face to the wall. She didn't look at us. I wanted to run and hang onto her skirt, but Andy wouldn't let go of my hand.

When the pastor came down, he was holding her hat. Daddy pulled it away. He pulled off the feathers. That was why I cried.

Andy pulled the cap off the telescope and pressed his face to the eyepiece. He opened his mouth when he did that and kind of twisted it—the concentration, I guess.

"What's so funny?" he said.

"You look worse than a gopher. And you're sticking your bum in my face."

He shuffled away. "There's a whole battalion out there. Calhesians, I think. They've got lasers and everything."

"Let me see."

"I'm the Commander," he said. "I get to see first."

Lightning snared the fields, though the house was still caught in the sun.

"They've opened fire!" Andy pulled away from the telescope, scurried to the top of the ladder and down. "Come on! They're gonna open the sonic blasts. We have to get to the guns!"

I paused at the telescope, but he'd jostled it in his retreat, and it was focused on the sill.

"Hannah!"

The thunder came.

I climbed down the ladder. Andy grabbed my arm. We ran down the hall, the stairs, through the kitchen and the back door, slammed it behind us. The rain began.

From the woodpile, I grabbed a stick. "Yee-haw!" Straddled it like a horse. The lawn was already soup. For a moment, Andy too forgot the invasion, and we chased each other in circles and kicked up the mud with oar hooves.

Lightning again.

"They're closer!"

We ran with our sticks, along the stone edge of the garden, and up to the fence. The grass was long there. We squatted, and the blades lapped over us.

Andy waved his arm. "Missiles at the ready, men!" He sneezed and we fired, though you couldn't hear it above the thunder.

The clouds were so close now I was frightened. Like gravy pitchers over our heads. But I wouldn't say anything. I wasn't going to hide under Andy's arm the way I did when I was little.

I bit my lip and kept saying, "Pow! Zam! Yap, yap, yap!" My feet went to sleep from squatting and I sat down suddenly and put my hand on something sharp. There was a break between thunder claps. Andy looked down at me.

"You okay?" He had the battle lust in his eyes: cheeks all pink and a little spit at the corner of his mouth from too many "pows!"

"I'm okay." I showed him my hand. The palm was pooling red. I swallowed. "I'm not okay, actually."

"They shot you," said Andy.

"No, I put my—" I tried not to look at it.

"They shot you." He stood up and pulled me beside him with his hands in my armpits. "Retreat!" he shouted. "Retreat to the bunker! Everyone follow me!"

We ran to the kitchen door, up through the yellow grass. The door wouldn't open. Sometimes it sticks in the wet.

"Follow me!" Andy waved his arms. "Around to the front, men!"

We ran around the side of the house, through the lawn full of thistles and up the steps to the front porch. Daddy wasn't there. My hand hurt. Now it really hurt.

Andy pulled on the door, but it wouldn't open. The front door never sticks. You have to slam it just to keep it closed.

"We're locked out," he said. "They must have infiltrated the base."

I held my hand away from my side, because I didn't want to get blood on my shirt. Andy sat down, and I sat down beside him.

"Show me your hand," he said. I did, and he looked at it for a while and then poked it so that I screamed. "Enemy shrapnel," he said. "You wanna see?"

I didn't want to, but I looked anyway, and there was a piece of porcelain with the pattern of a flower on the edge. Andy dropped the piece quick.

At the bottom of the steps, the rain filled the driveway potholes and overflowed. We sat and watched the puddles go from brown to clear, the mud settling to the bottom: surrender. Soon the worms would come out. Daddy's van wasn't there.

"He must have gone into town," said Andy.

"You mean the spaceport?"

"Town," he said.

I began to cry.

The next day, the foster workers came.

Andrew Battershill
here we are in santorini

i am 53 years old: on my
bright red acapulco shirt
tiny surfers
try to escape
their polyester prison.

i train a video camera
on my wife whose
glasses rest on her nose
their edges curling up into the sky.

she is giving her permed blond
hair that one little push
at the bottom
as if she can make it rise
into something bigger
something more important than hair.

is it on? she asks
the same tentative question she asks every time.

i tell her i can see
the red light so
she takes this in stride as she always does and

summons all the nasal energy of her voice to yell out
knowing that dozens
of family members and nail salon friends
will sit on our ragged couch
in the living room and
watch her stand stiff
give the performance
of a lifetime.

and most will go home
roll their eyes and try to forget
the musky smell caught in our
shag carpet
and some will rave
to their downtrodden spouses about how
glenda should be in pictures.

Danielle Ayotte
Leaving My Mother

The real reason we had to leave Quebec was my mother.

In the fall, the leaves were the same color as lipstick: Chinese red, and on some days, when the sun is somewhere else in the world, the shade turned them a burnt orange.

Teeth were the streetlights and stars: white oval shapes in the sky.

From the plane everything vanished, the Catholic churches, the gargoyles and brick houses, every piece of city disappeared like melting snow; I turned around, and it was gone.

When you're young, you do not have to hide your tears. I was six and cried over five provinces.

No one here is French. They laugh at my father's accent, our broken English. We mispronounce our *H*'s, over-pronounce our *R*'s. On the bus, my father rumbles with change while asking the driver, "We go to de market how?" The driver looks at him. "Market? You mean like a grocery store? For food?"

"Yes!" my father says enthusiastically. The driver begins giving him directions in a slow and almost sing-song voice— as if he were talking to a child, maybe even a baby monkey.

Here we are foreign enough to be different, but not foreign enough to be exotic.

Everything here is green—when there was no snow in December, I bawled. Angry and cheated, I stomped around our apartment in my snow boots and wore scarves and mittens even to bed.

When I refused to take them off, my father made me bathe in cold water. "I thought you would love the weather here," my father said in French, his voice quiet and apologetic, "there is not so much wind."

In Quebec, the air had become my mother's voice—on stormy days it would howl and scream at us. But here, it was rarely heard in more than a whisper. "Here," she tells us, "I am home."

There is only one French channel on the television set. My mother tells me that it is good, watching the other channels will improve my English. After she leaves the room, I will throw the remote against the wall.

My father has gotten a job at the Type and Write shop on Quadra Street. There he fixes typewriters behind a black counter. The only other employee is Robert Grant. He is the owner, the cashier and the bookkeeper.

In Quebec my father was a history professor. When I was still too young to go to school, my mother would take me to visit him at lunch. I would run up and down the stairs of the auditorium. Later, while sitting together on his desk, he and my mother would eat lunch and laugh. They would discuss British Columbia—moving luggage, elementary schools—my father would look sick. I pretended not to listen.

We didn't bring everything when we left. Mom said it would take up too much space in the apartment.

I hid in the closet until 13:04; then we had to leave for the airport. When we arrived, I discovered that even time was different here.

At night Papa dreams about Quebec. I can hear him.

Once I tiptoed into his room when I heard crying. "Papa," I had said, "what's wrong?" In the darkened room my father took my hand and placed it on his bare chest. "It is my heart, *ma petite citrouille*," he said, "it's broken."

Cities never leave you, even after you've turned your back and walked away. Eventually foreign trees turn into familiar ones— trees that you've seen before. Sidewalks change in the sun— Quebec's favorite weather. Even the perfume of strangers turns into the smell of smoke from vanilla cigarettes. It fills our lungs and makes us want to scream, *maison, interieur*.

My mother loves it here.

I wonder how many cities we'll have to visit before we can go home.

Vanessa Service
Tallroom Pantsing

My father is taking dancing lessons: tap or ballroom, we're not really sure which. He claims he's combined the two: Tallroom Pantsing...or was it Baltap Dancing? At any rate he also insists it's bound to be the next big spectator sport at the Olympics. My sister and I roll our eyes and never bother to argue. Question his knowledge of his newfound passion and you'll set him off on one of his rants about the curse of parenting and how he should have gotten a vasectomy twenty years ago. No, it's much better (and much more amusing) to let him do his thing.

I spy on him while he practices, whirling around the kitchen counting to himself: "one, two and three...one, two and three..."

He is constantly making up his own steps, juxtaposing scuffs with promenades, turning both left and right. Even crazier than these combinations are the names he comes up with for them: Jacuzzi. Slurpee. Rocking chair. All completely irrelevant but apparently (according to Dad) fit the movement. I suspect he just likes to say the words, enjoying how they themselves waltz off of his tongue. Why he even bothers going to the classes I'll never know, because the steps he learns there are so butchered and mis-matched the result has a somewhat Frankenstein essence. I'd almost classify it as graceful to see this middle-aged beer belly swirling about. Graceful in a hippo-type fashion, but graceful nonetheless.

Mom threatens that this absurd dancing around the kitchen will either give him indigestion or he'll poke someone's eye out with the chopsticks he hits on the counter to hold rhythm. Dad just keeps on spinning.

Angeline Wilde
Warranty

She felt them fall onto her hand in ones and twos and sometimes
four at a time. It was a familiar brush of tantalizing anxiousness,
leprosy of the mind or maybe this time, a cure. She emptied the
orange plastic bottle into her palm and closed it. Rolled each
dose in the clamminess of her skin, making their edges round
and hurt. She chose a pill carefully, whichever one looked most
enticing in the clouds' white light. She reached backward until
her shoulder blade rubbed the other and launched it into the
reaches of the blackberry bushes overlooking the highway's
rush-hour traffic.

Her body quavered a moment as she repositioned herself
on the curved peak of the slate-shingled roof. The breeze lifted
her shirt, and her pants sunk down from her awkward position.
She looked into the backyard. She stared at a concrete slab that
poked a rounded head out the long yellowing grass on the left.
The yard was bordered with thick, black, snowberry bushes. She
thought the enclosure was once a graveyard. There was an oak
that hung just far enough to shade one corner. Even in the dark,
she could make out a piece of orange carpet bunched up like a
skittish fox watching from a distance, its eyes in a hidden gaze
toward her. She reached for a pill and chucked it in fox's direction. The pill's velocity petered out about three feet away from
its claws. It didn't move. She got up and put a foot on either side
of the roof's crown. The wind blew a hard gust, and she watched
a group of leaves get pulled up, caught in circles in front of the
garage door on the other side of the house. She looked down at
the handful of softening capsules, which stuck to her skin as she
opened her fist.

The past two years had been nothing to her. She was the
type of person she thought she'd only humor, not become.

191

Before she lost her virginity to Geoffrey Munich, she thought there'd be some similarities with the person she was: a "very good" student, according to prefabricated report card comments. Number 5: *It is a pleasure to have this student in class.* Or Number 37: *Best is too small a word for this student.* She was someone no one hated but wouldn't really get to know. A girl who could walk around her house in spandex shorts and a tie-dyed hair band and her family wouldn't care. To her, late meant one o'clock in the morning, or the last bus that went past Jon's place. To her parents, her comments were only disrespectful if she was angry. She was the girl that bought new clothes but was never quite in fashion.

At Jon's apartment, about a fifteen-minute bus ride from Jen's house and twenty minutes from her own, the all-nighters were almost a guarantee. The exception being when someone who drove, an unlikely occurrence, was sober enough by 6:00 AM and, even less likely, to taxi her home. It was a mad rage of twix's, twists and turns with boys with twelve-hour warranties. If only it hadn't been Friday. Her mother cooked garlic bread and medium-rare steak with ketchup so she'd stay for dinner, because she knew that was her daughter's favorite. She rushed her mom to get it done, and she ate early, and if she hadn't, she wouldn't have taken the phone call from Jen. She wouldn't have sat by the toilet before brushing her teeth, to make sure her stomach was empty. Her eyes would have taken less time to color the Annabelle Midnight Blue with her finger. Her hair would have been left in a wavy half ponytail, instead of ironed down to her shoulders and around her small face. Her pants would have been fine without being shrunk in the dryer before leaving, and the black pair of underwear would never have been that much better than the white. She wouldn't have tripped over her dog on the way out or cared about bringing her Visine.

The apartment was three-quarters full when she and Jen arrived. They said hello to those they knew and pulled their mickeys out of Esprit bags, bought on the trip to Vancouver two weeks earlier. That was the time Jen walked into some ugly guy on the sidewalk, named Kai. "Watch it asshole," Jen had said.

She had laughed and ran across the street on the way back to the hotel. She watched, through passing cars, Kai point his finger at the Link's Bar sign two windows down the sidewalk. She watched Jen smile, looking at the sign and start walking toward it like a moth to light. She called the hotel at 8:00 AM the next morning. The girl had canceled their plans to have lunch with Mr. and Mrs. Kale, friends of her parents she met when she was five, who had wanted to see ten years of growth. Jen said she doesn't remember a thing.

After three shots and four more arrivals, three guys and a girl, she decided to meet the guests she didn't know. At first she watched and let the hum of the music massage the white lawn chair she'd chosen in the corner. She picked two guys in the kitchenette, both semi-reclining against the sink and the chipped stained cupboards. One blew out a puff of smoke. It dissipated slowly into the thick white air. "What's your name?" she asked. She thought this corner seemed more shielded from the sound than hers. The one with the red hat was named Julian; the cigarette boy was Geoff.

The next time she looked for Jen, her mickey was three-quarters finished. She felt her hand being tugged in one direction. She watched as it rose in the air and was pulled by Julian out the door. It had rained. They walked up the cement tile walk and rounded a corner to the side of the building, next to the AirWalk Garbage Disposal bins. She watched as the remnants of rain dripped inside from the gutters twenty feet above. She could almost smell its dark green shell slowly rusting with water and waste. She looked to where her hand was still cold, entrapped in Julian's. Geoff came around the corner and smiled. He asked her to hold his Kokanee. He put one hand on her side, his other hand and one of hers still holding the beer. She thought, for a moment, he would dance with her while Julian laughed, and they wouldn't care. He kissed her. "What about me?" She kissed Julian too. Her socks were a cold skin tight on her feet. Geoff lit a cigarette.

The pills were like mush now, a white paste in her hand. She could feel it getting warm. The wind blew another gust across the slate shingles encrusted in moss from the leaning oak tree. She flinched and shifted her weight from one leg to the other to stay upright. She scraped her hand along the curved peak of the roof to wipe it clean. She spread it like icing over the roughness, so the white covered the black slate. With her finger, she drew the fox in the corner. She could tell rush hour was almost over.

Michelle Andersen
Can She Begin to Forget About This
Empty Basement In Her Belly?

I know nothing of my history.

Do I have a mother
who eats cherries for breakfast,

four   biscuits   with   tea?

Maybe she spoke to me in Persian,
or sang Russian lullabye-byes
rocking me in my weathered cocoon.
No,
        I don't think so.

I didn't crawl out of the womb. /
    umbilical cord severed, juices leaking
                                    /someone PUSHED me.

There must have been a reason
        for not cutting off my

                life source

        before the *first trimester* (allows you to resume most of your
                        normal schedule within a day or two!)
        or did she wait till the second and shy away from
                the three-or four-day process of:

opening the cervix
lab tests
urine tests
pap test
surgery

"To minimize the strain to your cervical muscle you may undergo
gradual dilation that could
                              take a few hours or happen overnight."

Maybe the guilt was too much
        or she didn't want anything to touch her ever again.

Still, what about a pill?
                    MIFEPREX
                    (lovely name for a daughter isn't it?)
Could have swallowed my terracide for me,
taken it down with a tall glass of orange juice.

I've been told she didn't want to remain in contact with me.
                A choice on her own?

But,
        what gnaws at me the most:

Did I kill her?

Kristina Lucas
Cab Ride

November second, downtown
Victoria
(Yates and Government)
it's raining:

hail a taxi; the driver asks
where
you want to go.

says proudly he can take you anywhere.

you tell him
Eaton's Center,
Toronto
(August twenty-sixth,
2000).

fuck lady, that's four
years ago and halfway across the country!
what are you
crazy?

(not crazy, just
late).

you apologize, ask if he can take you
to the
airport.

yeah, he can do that

pulls away from the curb, you
look

at your watch, swear it is
a few years
fast;

wonder

how long you would wait
drinking food-court coffee
(watered down and
overpriced)

to see a daughter
whose name you would want to
forget

if you knew it.

Alan Orr
In Search of a Plot

When Jimmy awoke that Saturday morning, he knew instantly that something was wrong. Well, not wrong exactly, but different. Nothing in his room had changed; his clothes were still lying on and over everything. The hands of his Mickey Mouse clock were still glowing faintly in the gloom; the carpet was still dingy. But somehow, Jimmy knew something had changed.

Uncertainly, he sat up and swung his legs over the side of the bed. He rubbed his eyes, yawned, scratched his—

"Hey!"

What?

"Do you really need to tell everyone that? And what's with this vague, pitiful 'something's different!' crap?"

It's foreshadowing.

"You mean I'm in a story?"

A short one.

"Oh, great. Thanks a bunch. So I'm in a story—that's what's different?"

Yes, now get on with the plot.

"You're the narrator. Give me one."

No.

"What? Look, man, you can't just—"

Jimmy got up.

"Hey!"

He ambled sleepily down the short hall into the living room, wondering again what fool architect had put the bathroom on the other side of it. The rug was spotless, as always, the two couches and the end table neat and artistically arranged. Damn roommates of his couldn't leave a nice mess alone. They were away for the weekend, and yet Jimmy still

199

couldn't mess things up, since they'd flay him alive if anything was out of place when they came back.

"Want to stay out of my life? Thanks."

The shower was cold at first but was soon steaming. A hot shower always woke him up and helped him think.

His job as a story character required him to work all kinds of strange hours, but he hadn't been ready for this. He normally worked in novels or screenplays, both of which allowed even the main character to take his time with the plot. That, and the fact that most narrators provided a plot, meant a short story came as a bit of a shock.

What shall my plot be? he wondered, and then thought, that narrator's reading my mind, isn't he?

Well, what do I know about short stories?

Not a lot. Especially now that the first page was almost finished—it would be difficult to work anything in this late. Jimmy was experienced, but he wasn't a miracle worker.

"Okay. Look. I'm willing to work with you but you gotta help me out. I need a plot," Jimmy proclaimed to the air as he shut off the water and stepped out of the shower.

Why should I?

"Because we've already gone on for too long without one. At least provide a hook."

There was a pause.

"Quit stalling."

But only silence answered his plea.

"Jerk."

Jimmy dried off, knowing that sometimes one must simply put one's trust in fate. "Whatever," he muttered. When he was dry he wrapped a towel around himself and opened the bathroom door. Four steps into the living room he stopped in his tracks.

There was a corpse lying in his living room. And not just any corpse—this one was mutilated. Deep gashes were visible through the ragged torn street clothing of what had once been a middle-aged bearded man.

Jimmy slapped his forehead. "You vindictive, sadistic son of a—"

A pickax lay on the floor by the body.

"You're not helping. My roommates are going to lynch me."

And a large corkscrew.

Jimmy made a noise of disgust in his throat and went over to the small table by the couch. He picked up the cordless phone and dialed 9-1-1. A woman's voice answered, deliberately calm and slightly bored.

"Hello, please state your emergency."

"Hi, I need the police. There's a, um...a dead body in my living room."

"Are you all right, sir?"

"My narrator's screwing with me, but yeah, I'm fine."

"Sir?"

"Long story. Can you get somebody over here?"

"A squad car is on its way."

"Thanks. Should I stay on the line?"

"Yes please, sir. Our psychologist would like a word with you."

"What? Psychologist?"

"Yes, sir." The voice was still a woman's, but a different woman's, clipped and professional. Six years of schooling. "Just a few questions. I believe you mentioned a narrator?"

"Yeah. See, I work as a story character, and my narrator for this job is kind of a...well, we're not getting along."

"Can you describe your...narrator?"

"Uh...not really. He's bodiless and omnipresent." Jimmy was beginning to feel uneasy. "There, did you catch that?"

"Sir?"

"Did you catch that? My narrator just said that I was feeling uneasy."

"I'm sorry, I didn't hear anything. And don't be afraid of your feelings."

"Right. He must only be using limited omniscient, the slippery bastard. Look, are we almost finished?"

"Hmm? Oh, yes, nearly. Is there a history of insanity in your family?"

"Nothing comes to mind."

"I'll bet."

Jimmy heard the scrunch of tires in the gravel driveway.

"You shut up," snapped Jimmy.

"Pardon, sir?"

"Nothing. Police are here, gotta go."

Jimmy hung up and descended the stairs, still in his towel, rubbing his forehead and letting out his breath in exasperation. "Weirdest damn job I've ever taken...," he muttered to himself. Through the glass door he could see the distorted outlines of two people. He opened it to reveal two large burly police officers.

"Burly is right," he gulped, eyes wide.

One of them raised an eyebrow, making his face look like a skeptical cinderblock.

"Never mind, for God's sake," said Jimmy, shaking his head. "Come on in, the body's upstairs."

"Actually, sir, we need you to come with us."

"What for? Is the killer still here or something? Now, that would be a good plot—a slasher! I've never done one of those."

The second officer sniggered. The twist of an ominous realization began to manifest itself in Jimmy's gut.

He swallowed. "You're right for once," he choked out.

One of the officers commented to the other, "You're right. Bonkers."

"Quite mad," the other agreed gravely.

And as they took Jimmy by the arms and began to drag him away, Jimmy cried out:

"Damn you! Damn you, I say!"

To the world and cruel, cruel fate he cried out, to the indifferent and merciless gods of—

"No, you bastard, I'm talking to you! I'm coming for you, you poor excuse for an omnipotent being! I'll find out where you live! I'll cut ya! *I'll cut ya!*"

"Sad how it takes hold so quick," the first officer remarked regretfully.

"And in one so young, too," agreed the other.

Sad, indeed.

Kathleen Aitken
The way she folded the laundry: a palindrome

He loved her
but he couldn't find a way to tell her
between the bite of zippers and Velcro,
mismatched socks and underwear.
He was under siege.
She was throwing them at him;
she wasn't folding them anymore.
Raising the hair on the back of his neck,
he felt the static jump up her arm
as she separated the cotton from polyester.
She only grabbed another wrinkled shirt,
she couldn't look at him,
brittle, quivering with suppressed screams,
the way she folded the laundry.

The way she folded the laundry
Was brittle, quivering with suppressed screams.
She couldn't look at him.
She could only grab another wrinkled shirt
separated the cotton from polyester
and feel the static jump up her arm
to raise the hair on the back of his neck,
and soon she wasn't folding them anymore
she was throwing them, at him.
He was under siege
of mismatched socks and underwear.
And between the bite of zippers and Velcro,
he couldn't find a way to tell her,
that he loved her.

Kyra Benloulou
Should Be Writing Spanish Essay

Right now,
ahora mismo,
I want you,
in Spanish class,
right under the nose of the teacher.
Boy, all it would take to get you
and me into the bathroom next door
is a note, discreetly passed,
hand slipped below desk
to thigh, and then just a little higher.
But no, you took psychology and
right now,
ahora mismo,
you are learning about human desire,
instead of feeling it cast its dark, inviting feathers.

Peggy Hogan
Pantoum for a Setting Sun

> *Chance that a Japanese grade-school student reports never having seen a sunrise or sunset: 1 in 2.*
> —HARPER'S INDEX

Village fishermen tell tales of pink skies,
seas of *sakana* thick as Tolstoy's novels,
silk paintings of nets bulging.
I am ten, I know nothing.

Seas of *sakana* thick as Tolstoy's novels.
Two hours a day I spend with books,
I am ten, I know nothing,
I don't stop to see the sky.

Two hours a day I spend with books.
I am restless, like papers carried by the wind.
I don't stop to see the sky,
time tight as a virgin.

I am restless. Papers carried by the wind
are swept up in *o soji*.
Time tight as a virgin
runs past familiar faces in store windows.

Swept up in *o soji*,
I frown over lost minutes,
run past familiar faces in store windows
and return home to teal textbooks.

I frown over lost minutes,
the dimming light in the west.
Teal textbooks suddenly don't hold answers:
how it feels to see stoplight-red on the horizon.

Losing light to the west,
I cannot imagine sunsets—
a stoplight-red flame over the horizon.
I am ten, I know nothing.

o soji—the daily cleaning of the school which every Japanese student participates in

sakana—fish

Max Bell
June

Memorial Arena is a strange place for a tenth anniversary, but Bob and June have a bit of a strange history. Bob's fifteen minutes early, and although June's consistently late, he's not worried. The Bauers he's had under the stairs since his last year of minor hockey take at least ten minutes to tie. Plus, he'll have to rent June a pair. He knots his fraying laces and crosses the lobby's gray carpet to the Skate Shop. The blond behind the cash register smiles and takes his collection of change, hands him back a pair of ladies' fives, winks a blue eye. Bob forces a smile back but thinks only of June.

Before June, Bob would never have thought about ice-skating. In fact, before June, Bob never thought about much of anything. He didn't need to. May, his fiancée, did the thinking for him. A redhead hell-bent on marriage knows all the answers, any man will tell you that. The day Bob ate lunch with May in the Eaton's Center food court, he didn't think much either. As he walked two steps behind May (close enough to please, far enough to ignore), he caught the auburn eyes of June from across the room. And even though May was already on the escalator, halfway down to Douglas Street, Bob knew he wasn't going anywhere. June always comes after May. He didn't think twice.

Michelle Morris
Cow in the Yard

When my neighbor knocked on my door for the first time, I was baking cookies and singing. The song was from this movie my girlfriend had made me watch with her; the film had actually turned out to be good. It was a musical, and though I would never admit it, I had a secret love for musicals. So when my neighbor knocked, I was practically shouting, I was so into the song. It was hard to stop in the middle like that to answer the door.

The first thing she said to me was, "There's a cow in your yard."

"What?" I said.

"Cow. In your yard. I would have phoned you but my phone's not working." She was looking at my hand, which held a spatula. I was looking at her, trying to figure out why she, who was a stranger to me, would be at my door.

"Who are you?" I said.

"Jan. Your neighbor to the north. I work at night, that's why you haven't seen me."

"I'm Brynn. Where do you work?" I opened the door wider for her to come in.

"I'm a nurse."

"Come into the kitchen. I was just making cookies. You can have some if you're still here when they're ready."

"About the cow...," she said.

"Cow? Oh yeah."

"I saw it go into your yard, so I thought I'd tell you, in case you had a vegetable garden or something, but my phone's down, and the company said it would be a week before they fixed it, and I don't think I know your number anyway. That's why I'm here."

"I haven't planted anything yet," I said, "but thanks for letting me know."

Jan watched silently while I measured flour, baking soda and salt. I started singing again. "To loving tension, no pension. To more than one dimension. To starving for attention hating convention hating pretension." Jan was taking the eggs out of the carton I had left open on the table and balancing them on their ends in a neat row. "La vie bohème," I sang, plucking an egg from the end of Jan's row and cracking it on the edge of the sink. The eggs came from an old couple down the street. I'd even seen the chickens, pecking and squawking around the yard.

"So, what do I do about the cow?" I asked.

"Its people will come and get it eventually. Probably it's the same one that came through here last time. Some of them just can't stay inside the fence."

I realized too late that I had been mixing eggs and not looking at Jan while she was talking. My girlfriend hates it when I do that. I sneaked a look at Jan, but she didn't seem too annoyed.

"There's a squirrel outside," I said. "Don't you love how they run? Like they're just floating. And their tail does this little wavy thing—it's neat."

I guessed Jan was one of those people who doesn't feel the need to say something every time you say something, because she didn't say anything. But she did get up and look at the squirrel.

Jan helped make little balls of dough, all spherical and uniform. None of mine were as perfect, and Jan kept moving them into straighter rows, but I didn't care. I put the cookie sheet in the oven, and Jan set the timer. It was amazing that she'd figured out how. You have to press OVEN, then TIMER, before turning the dial.

Someone knocked on the door while we were washing our hands. I ran to answer it, and Jan scampered behind me, like we were kids or something. It was my second stranger of the day, this one clad in muddy rubber boots and jeans. "We've come to get our cow," she said.

Jan and I went for a walk. There used to be an elementary school near where we lived, but, Jan explained, there hadn't been enough kids in recent years so they shut it down. Now the school building belonged to a church, but the playground, soccer field and basketball nets were still there. We stopped for a swing.

I started thinking about that movie I saw with my girlfriend, the musical. It was called *Rent*. At the end, most of the characters have a girlfriend or a boyfriend, except one. After the movie, my girlfriend kept talking about him; she felt sorry for him, she said. All alone. But I liked the ending. Movies where everything ends up being absolutely perfect just aren't believable.

I jumped off the swing. The playground had one of those bouncy things where kids sit on each end, like a teeter-totter, only more springy. I got on and started bouncing. Secretly, I was hoping Jan would join me, because those bouncy things are better with two people. My girlfriend never goes on them with me—she thinks they're for kids. But if Jan agreed with my girlfriend, she didn't say, just silently climbed on.

We both walked back to my house, and I put cookies on a plate for Jan. "I haven't got any paper ones, so you'll have to give this back when you're done," I said, piling cookies on a ceramic dish.

"There's a message on your machine," Jan said. "May I use your washroom?" It's funny when people change the subject like that without a breath in the middle. It's like they had two thoughts to say and couldn't decide which one was more important.

I pressed the message button when I heard the bathroom door shut.

"Hi, it's me," said my girlfriend, her voice slightly tinny from the machine. I wished she would say her name, in case I get her mixed up with my sister or someone. Voices aren't as distinctive on the phone. "I went to the SPCA yesterday and they had really cute puppies. They were spaniel and something else, I forget, but really friendly and not too noisy. Anyway, I thought I could take you down to see them before they're all gone. Call back. Bye."

"I don't want a puppy," I told the machine. I pressed erase, and wrote myself a note on the white board on my fridge: *Puppies.* My sister had been given the white board in high school to stick in her locker. In our family, there was an unspoken rule that if you didn't want something you'd put it in someone else's bedroom, and that's what my sister had done. She'd left it underneath a stack of old comic books. I didn't find it until I was packing to move out and putting the comics in her room, under her old stuffed animals in the closet.

Jan shuffled back into the kitchen. "I'll go. You can phone whoever it was back."

"You don't have to go."

"Everything shows on your face, did you know?"

"It doesn't."

Jan shrugged.

"I told my girlfriend I wanted a pet, and she wants me to go look at puppies."

"So?"

"She wants me to get one. I don't like puppies. I don't want to argue about whether anyone can dislike puppies."

"Do you love your girlfriend?"

"What kind of question is that?"

"I'm sorry."

Jan put on muddy runners, double knotted them, and left. Of course I love my girlfriend, I was thinking. Otherwise she wouldn't be my girlfriend. The problem was, lately it seemed like she didn't understand me anymore. She kept forgetting things, like the fact that I didn't like puppies. The other day we had eaten dinner at her house. Chicken, which she knew I didn't like. Last week at a café she had ordered me a coffee. "No, I'll have hot chocolate," I said. She said, "What are you talking about?" I explained to her that I didn't like coffee, never had. She frowned and refused to believe me.

I took the eggs back out of the fridge. I tried every egg in the carton. On the table, the counter, even the floor, but none would stay on end. I gave up when one rolled off the table and broke.

I went with my girlfriend to the SPCA to look at the puppies. They were cute, I admit it, but I didn't want one. My girlfriend watched as they trotted about their cage, tripping on each other, biting, yipping, panting, just being cute. "You should get that one," she whispered. The puppy wasn't doing much, but its long hair was glossy and its eyes were bright. Every so often it would wag its tail. I thought of the long hair weaving its way into my living room carpet, its bright eyes begging forgiveness for chewing my shoes.

"You should get that one," I said.

"I should?" She looked at me. Maybe this thought was not new to her.

"I think maybe I'll get a bird. I don't want a dog. But I might like a bird."

"Okay."

My girlfriend brought two puppies home, so they'd keep each other company, she said. One of them kept trying to eat the living room carpet. The other had a passion for peanut butter: I once ate peanut butter before visiting my girlfriend, and the dog kept following me around and licking my hands. My girlfriend thought it was hilarious.

However, she didn't want to go back to the SPCA with me.

"It's so depressing there," she said. I agreed but wanted her to go there again with me. I wanted my own pet.

This is how I found myself at Jan's front door. I didn't know her phone number, so I couldn't phone her or anything. After knocking, I remembered she worked night shift. But she answered the door. "I thought you worked night shift," I said. "Did I wake you up?"

"I have some time off right now. I sort of sleep when I'm tired and get up when I wake up. But if you thought I would be sleeping, why did you knock on my door?"

"I forgot until I knocked. Do you want to go to the SPCA with me? I need a pet."

"Didn't you go with your girlfriend?"

"Yeah, but we got puppies for her and no pets for me."

"More than one puppy?"

"She thought just one would get lonely."

"Okay. I'll get my coat." She gave me a puzzled look. I wasn't sure why.

We went into the room labeled SMALL ANIMALS. I looked at the birds. They ignored me. Three people came in with a cage. Wood shavings on the floor of the cage were sculpted into hills. One hill moved.

"What's in there?" I asked.

"Gerbils," said the girl carrying the cage. "Want to hold one?"

"Sure."

The woman with SPCA on her shirt checked to see the door of the room was closed. The girl reached in and pulled a gerbil out of the wood shavings. "This is Lena." She put Lena in my hand and petted her head.

Lena was beautiful in a rat-like way. She didn't demand that you admire her soft glossy fur, but you could if you wanted to. I brought Lena and her sister Tibby home with me.

My girlfriend arrived at my house unexpectedly. "I got off work early today," she explained. "The power went out, and we phoned BC Hydro and they said it wouldn't be back for hours. So everyone left."

"That's great. Sorry, but I'm kind of in the middle of putting a bookshelf together. I'll be done in just a moment, though."

She followed me back to my bookshelf upstairs. "I wonder what a cow that got out of its pen would be thinking. I mean, would it be happy, like, 'Yay, I'm free!' or just lost and confused?"

My girlfriend smiled and didn't answer. She went downstairs, and I returned my attention to the bookshelf. It was one of those things that come with ready-made pieces, which you put together yourself. The instructions, I'm sure, had been translated from Japanese to German to Swedish to English, getting hopelessly mangled in the process. Fortunately, it didn't seem to be too difficult. I was glad I hadn't bought something complicated like a bunk bed with drawers. My sister had one of those when she was a kid. We had to hire some guy to put it together for us.

When I returned from my bookshelf, Jan was in the living room with my girlfriend. She had a habit of inviting herself in whenever she felt like it. "Hi, Jan."

"Can I hold your gerbils?"

Jan put the gerbils on the coffee table. "Don't put them there!" I said. She moved them to the couch. My girlfriend watched her with suspicion.

"How long have you two known each other?" my girlfriend asked.

"Since the day the cow got into his yard," Jan answered.

"A cow got into your yard? Does this happen often?" My girlfriend was probably wondering why I had moved out to farm country.

Jan said, "Can I make some hot chocolate?"

"Go for it. Make some for me too."

"None for me," my girlfriend said.

We watched Jan deposit the gerbils on my lap and disappear into the kitchen.

"Why is she here?" my girlfriend whispered.

I shrugged. "She comes over to visit sometimes. I think she's kind of lonely. She mostly works night shift, and she doesn't see a lot of people when she sleeps all day."

"She's awake now."

"It's the weekend. She didn't work last night. And she doesn't sleep all day every day."

Lena hopped onto my girlfriend's knee, startling her. "It's okay," I said. "You can pet her if you want. Slowly. Just with one finger." Lena scampered away from my girlfriend's outstretched finger. "They don't usually like to be petted; it's worth a try, though."

"These gerbils just don't like me."

"They just need some time to get used to you. They haven't decided if they like you yet. But you could hurt them, so it's safer for them to be cautious."

"They like Jan."

"She takes them out more."

"You mean she's here more."

"No! But when she is here, she usually takes the gerbils out, and you usually don't."

Jan came in then. "A squirrel tried to get into your birdfeeder," she said. "It took a huge flying leap at the roof, landed on it and slid right off. It was pretty funny." She set a cup of hot chocolate down in front of me.

I picked up the gerbils. "I should put Tibby and Lena away."

I knew my girlfriend would be glaring at Jan while I wasn't in the room, and Jan would be drinking her hot chocolate nonchalantly.

Tibby and Lena tried to come back out of their cage. "Later," I promised them.

In the living room Jan was humming quietly. I sat down, picked up my hot chocolate and watched the mug fall into my lap. It bounced off my knee onto the floor, where it shattered. Hot chocolate was everywhere. I was thankful that Jan makes hot chocolate the way I like it: hot, but not hot enough to burn your tongue, or, evidently, the rest of you. I stood up and dripped hot chocolate onto the rug.

"I'll get a cloth," my girlfriend said.

"In the kitchen, the drawer beside the door," I told her and Jan. They went to get one. I stepped out of my pants and left them in a chocolate puddle on the floor. Then I ran upstairs before anyone could see me.

"How did you drop it?" my girlfriend asked when I was back downstairs in my second pair of pants for the day.

"I dunno. It just slipped, I guess." Carefully, I picked up bits of mug. "I mean I wasn't planning on it or anything." I realized I had hot chocolate on my shirt too. I took the pieces of porcelain into the kitchen; then I went upstairs to change my shirt.

I closed the door to my bedroom, and a piece of paper whooshed up off the floor. I picked it up. *Cinema 2*, it said, 7:20 PM *Rent*. I put the ticket on my desk.

I put some more chocolate milk on the stove to heat up and started singing. My mom always sang when she was cooking, so maybe that's why I do. I took another dish towel into the living room.

"What is that song about?" Jan asked.

"*La vie bohème*? It's about everything in life that is good, even when not everything works out. In the movie, the bad guy is antagonizing the protagonists, saying their carefree way of life is over, and then they start singing this song." I took my hot chocolate-filled dish towel into the laundry room and then went back to the kitchen to stir the milk. I wanted to keep singing, and I didn't want to sing in the quiet living room with Jan and my girlfriend watching. I stuck my finger in the hot chocolate to see if it was warm enough. Not yet.

There was a large bird on the lawn outside the kitchen window. It had long striped tail feathers, a shiny green head and a white band around its neck. But the most startling thing was how shiny it was compared to all the other birds I'd seen around my yard. "Come look at this," I yelled into the living room.

My girlfriend and Jan came and stood on either side of me. "That's a pheasant," Jan said. "It belongs to these people up the road. We should catch it for them."

"Just leave it a minute," I said.

The pheasant strutted around the yard, head bobbing down to snap up fallen birdseed, tail floating like a banner.

I started singing again, quietly, still watching the pheasant. I couldn't tell if it was Jan or my girlfriend or both who joined in. When did you learn the words? I almost said. Instead, I kept singing.

Kaitlyn Boone
God and Me

cause you see, god and me, we real cool. we touch hands when we pass
in the halls and it's like a firebrand on my palm and we read joyce out
loud when it's cold and damn, ulysses ain't got nothing on me. and
what you got to know about god is she's all hair and hips and hands
and she's got a mouth like a sailor and a tongue like a siren.

we went to this bar that played jazz and served bad imperials to boys
that wanted to be men and god wore some low-cut black thing and
caustic heels that burned a cinnamon trail in every pizzicato footstep.
we were broke by the time we got there and i don't know if it was the
beggars or the acid that burned holes in our pockets but i had no idea
god could dance like that. she burned the wood floor like a watercolor
avalanche and shit you think god's powerful but you ain't got no idea
until you see that chick steal heartbeats. she played stravinsky with
her limbs and vodka shots, for the men at least, and for the boys she
played a modern aphrodite and their chests were her tempo, faster
when she fell into her curves, stopping altogether when her ice blues
collided with their pryings, ba bum, ba bum. she got off on their stares,
the way they mapped out her body, the way they traded cash in
hallways for ownership of her parts like she was real estate, and the one
who claimed her tits first declared victory but we all know the boy who
got her lips was the real winner.

she preferred raspberries to money and goddamn had her arms full by
the time the boys were drunk on her sticky breath. when she couldn't
dance anymore she'd fall into my chest but nearly miss and we'd be a
tense crimson for a moment. then she'd come to and peel herself off my
skin and drip in her hot vodka breath that i should kiss her. it would
rain and i knew it was her, wanting to get closer to me, massaging my

back in water and fingertips and letting a single hot tear run down my neck. like god would remember this tomorrow.

except maybe she would and would never say anything and throw a crumpled up napkin at me at lunchtime. and after classes she'd pretend like there wasn't a long bruise on her left thigh from the man who thought he knew so much, but her shoulder blades told me vulnerability and she bore them like imperfect wings.

Beth Davies
Statue

In Venice, the bull.

The car horns shouting
at staring, laughing faces.

Four oil-gray pigeons
squat to talk,
dulcet voices
lewd.

The bull stands,
chalky flank branded
by the black, dripping touch
of civilization.
How silently he stands,
how still

as the crowds murmur always,
the engines hum their off-key dirge,
and the pigeons snigger softly.

In Venice, the bull.
Stony eyes watch
the lives stroll by below,
the pop cans rattling
against his mighty hooves.

The pedestal, the prison
and moored to it
by his very substance,
the bull.

Michelle Morris
Hot Chocolate

I sit in Cassandra's kitchen and drink
hot chocolate, homemade with milk
and dark cocoa. I used to think
fancy hot chocolate came in a package
with artificial flavoring. Now I know
better, the way a small bird
leaves her cage, once, accidentally,
and feels the need to leave again.

When we were ten, I wanted
to teach grade one; wanted an uncomplicated life,
simple things: worksheets and show-and-tell,
spelling tests. Cassandra wanted to be
an astronaut; walk on Mars and
fly down a black hole,
see what was there.

Now, Cassandra talks quantum physics:
string theory, time
having no boundaries, no
beginning or end. This
is the only thing
in her scientific musings
that makes sense to me: the possibility
that this kitchen will always be here,
rock collection warming on the windowsill,
green grapes on the countertop,
one watering can on top of the refrigerator;
Cassandra, with her science,
stirring hot chocolate on the stove.

Chelsea Comeau
My Brother and Robert Pickton

When they found parts of my sister Charlene scattered across Robert Pickton's pig farm, my younger brother Jason was eleven years old. He and I understood exactly what death meant because we had killed our goldfish Craig when we tried to show him the intricate workings of a garburator.

Our mother seemed indifferent when we read Charlene's name. She was near the bottom of Pickton's list; he had been killing them for a very long time. Somehow I don't think Mum was very surprised because Charlene had always been the type of First Nations girl depicted on syndicated episodes of *To Serve and Protect*: drunk before nightfall, thighs choked by a pair of fishnet stockings. By the third time she was arrested for prostitution, we stopped crawling out of bed to pick her up at the police station and just let her deal with it herself.

Sasha and Tamara, our sisters, did not understand why I was crying. Jason went outside to throw rocks at the neighbor's dog, eventually paralyzing the thing when he struck it between the eyes. This was his first eruption of violence that I can remember.

I sat next to Mum with my clammy palm resting on her knee. It was bare, because she was wearing her favorite pair of striped shorts, and she listened to the spaniel next door as it howled in agony. She reached up to tuck a wisp of her auburn hair behind one ear and mumbled something about making dinner.

My hands felt awkward, as if they should have been doing something, but I couldn't think of what that something might be. I wiped my face with the cuff of my sleeve and tried to think clearly so that I could cling to something I understood beyond any shadow of a doubt.

I knew that I hadn't seen Charlene in many weeks and that now she was dead.

I knew that some perverted farmer in Port Coquitlam was probably responsible.

But I also knew that we would never have to listen to Charlene when she staggered home at three o'clock in the morning, breath sour and smelling like whiskey.

If I didn't think about how she had been mixed in with a plastic bucket of pig slop, I was actually quite relieved.

It has been four years since we first ate macaroni without saving a bowl of it for Charlene.

Jason is now fifteen. He wears a red Native Pride hat to school every day because he wants everyone to know that we are Haida and that we attend Aboriginal ceremonies; our grandfather is the chief of a band on Vancouver Island.

We are both enrolled at Windermere Secondary School, and we are driven there every day in a red '84 Tercel that smells like vanilla shampoo. On this particular morning, Jason is listening to a yellow Discman as he struts away without thanking Mum for the ride. He hums a Jim Morrison tune under his breath, and his jeans drag through a milky puddle at the edge of the parking lot. I cast Mum an apologetic glance, slinging my arms through the padded straps of my orange bag, shoulders hunched against the bracing November breeze. She wishes me good luck on an algebra test that I have barely studied for, then vanishes.

I shuffle my sneakers slowly. I am in the twelfth grade, and no one cares if you're five minutes late when you're getting ready to graduate. Nevertheless, I've generally tried to practice punctuality and impressive study habits, because I depend on scholarships to become a journalist.

Jason's future will be nothing like mine. His is a quagmire of uncertainty, because he likes to split lips and tell his teachers to fuck off. They just stare at him with watery eyes, oozing pity from their pores like sweat. They mumble excuses for him and let him slide through relatively unscathed, because our sister is dead, and no one wants to punish a child whose sister has been eaten by pigs.

When Jason hurls a textbook at the blond girl who cracks native jokes, they blame Pickton. When he cushions his fist with some pimply kid's nose, it's completely Robert's fault.

I would like to tell you that Jason is going to pull himself together when he fails math for the third time, but I refuse to hold my breath. I just don't have the lung capacity for it.

Maybe you need to know this, or maybe you don't, but on this particular day, when Jason drags his jeans through a puddle and hums a Jim Morrison song, his denim jacket is absorbing fat droplets of rain and becoming heavy. He shrugs it off before disappearing into the shop wing.

I can relax; today he is going to class instead of chain-smoking joints behind the school and facing another brief suspension that our mother doesn't have the time to deal with.

The shop is a separate concrete tomb where an arc welder hums Gregorian chants and circular saws shriek a soprano accompaniment. It is an awkward tune, but a tune that pacifies Jason. I think that the unpredictability of these dangerous implements is soothing for him.

I linger outside with a Newport in hand. My cousin sent a carton of these menthol treasures from a corner store in Seattle, and I want to fade away in the smell of them before immersing myself in the panic of photography class. The annual's blueprints need to be finished by the end of the week and sent off for printing, so everyone is a tangle of frayed nerves. The first bell rings, and I snuff the smoldering end of my cigarette, flicking it into the grass.

There are a hundred things to do before second period, and my stomach is gnawing at itself ferociously. I haven't had breakfast today.

Nearly half the morning has disintegrated in a tray of developing fluid.

I drown what will soon be a black and white portrayal of my mother, poking at the photo paper with a pair of plastic tongs. Her slack-shouldered image manifests slowly at first, a process that is dissolution in reverse. There are tiny pouches of loose skin beneath her hazel eyes, crow's-feet that bleed into deeply set forehead wrinkles.

Behind her, I can see our family's photo album on the coffee table and feel myself cringe. Those are the real pictures, the ones where all five of us are smiling on park benches. They're the ones where Jason isn't scowling at the lens, and where Charlene is still standing beside me with her arm slung casually around my waist.

This is how I like to remember them.

I like to think of Charlene as the girl who kept photographs of our father in a Nike shoebox underneath her bed.

He was a ghost of a man, who loved the woman he married more than he could ever love our mother. Charlene's photos of him were portals to the details of our genetic structure. Through glossy frozen flashbacks, we came to realize that we shared his coal-dust hair and sharp cheekbones, that our shoulders mimicked the same broad reach as his. But he had moved to a reserve in northern British Columbia, which may as well have been another country in comparison to our crowded Vancouver basement suite.

I knew that our mother had loved him zealously and in a desperate way, because she let him pass between her and the woman he married, never asking him to choose. She would disappear in the middle of the night to meet him at the stoop of a cheap motel, knowing that he would not come to our house. He didn't want to know that bastard replicas of him existed anywhere. His indiscretions were always without consequence.

After Charlene vanished for good, I tried to speak to him on the phone. I dialed the long-distance number that was scribbled on the back of a cocktail napkin, a number my mother had memorized but would never actually use. When he answered, our distant voices were separated by a steady crackling noise. The moment I told him who I was and blurted what had happened to his eldest daughter, he hung up.

Jason was standing next to me when I put the phone down. He slumped like a lung that's been poked by a shattered rib.

"He didn't want to talk to me?"

I winced. There was hope in his tone. The same desperation Mum must have felt each and every time she met with him. Jason wanted nothing more than to hear our father's voice. Even a shred of validation might have satiated him.

I extended my arms, tried to gather him up like scrambled puzzle pieces. He shrugged me off and shuffled to his bedroom. Had his rage been tangible, it would have hovered above him like a storm cloud pregnant with rain.

I have decided that if Jason were to leave, this is how I would remember him.

The smell of chemicals is beginning to give me a headache, and I emerge from the darkroom blinking frantically. There is always that brief instant of panic where I think that maybe my eyes will never readjust themselves and that I will be blind forever.

Mrs. Adwar is suddenly standing next to me, and she puts a hand on my shoulder before I can even make out the contours of her face. When she leans to murmur something into my ear, she reeks of eucalyptus cough drops, and as my pupils begin to function again, I think that I can see the mole on her left cheek sprouting a new hair.

"You need to report to the office right away," she tells me softly. "Take your bag with you."

The funny thing about bad news is that you can feel it hovering over you like the heavy scent of a grilled cheese sandwich that's starting to burn.

I shuffle the length of an empty corridor, radiant faces of past graduates beaming down ethereally at me. They are superficial and hopelessly optimistic. I wonder how many of them are greeters at Wal-Mart or flip beef patties at Burger King.

The plump secretary, whose calves hang limply over the lips of her brown loafers, glances in my direction but offers me no explanation. She has photographs of an orange cat framed on her desk and speaks with a thick Texan drawl.

I sit down on the black swivel chair that rests between the counselor and principal's offices. A pink rabbit's foot dangles from my key chain, and I fidget with it anxiously, trying to concentrate on the flawlessness of the combed fur.

"Michelle?" Mr. Davies, the principal, peers out from the bowels of his chamber. A pair of wire-rimmed glasses is perched at the end of his hooked nose, and I think that this is probably what an owl would look like if it morphed into a human. The caramel suit that stretches over his swollen gut is etched with a feathery diamond pattern. "Please, come inside and have a seat."

I drag my backpack across the purple carpet, let it rest at my sneakered feet as I lean back in the armchair he has offered to me. Mr. Davies has a very cramped office and seems to fill it more with his squealing laughter than his meaty calves.

Fortunately, he is not a word-mincer. "Jason has been arrested," he tells me, hands clasped loosely.

I begin to laugh. This is obviously a mistake because Jason went to class this morning, and I saw him do this with my very own eyes.

Mr. Davies' face has darkened, and he proceeds to elaborate. He explains to me that Constable Anderson tackled Jason to the floor and clamped handcuffs round his wrists.

I do not ask him why.

He waits for me. Realizes that I am unable to speak. Continues hesitantly.

A boy named Anthony was standing at the back of the room, talking about Robert William Pickton. He said that the women whose jigsaw leftovers were found on the farm deserved to be there. Especially the native ones.

I try to swallow the dryness in my throat because I know that this would have infuriated Jason. My cheeks flare a vibrant red, and I begin to tug at a loose thread on my sweatpants.

"So what did he do?"

Mr. Davies clears his throat. He cannot even look at me. He tells the story to the shelf of books behind me.

"He took a hammer from the wall."

Now I am not listening. I don't want to hear what Mr. Davies is telling the bookshelf.

I can't imagine what the leather-bound dictionary must be thinking when Mr. Davies says that Jason split the boy's temple open. It probably assumes that Mr. Davies is lying because things like this just don't happen. Boys don't hit other boys with hammers. Farmers don't feed prostitutes to their pigs.

The green collection of Shakespearean sonnets cringes because Mr. Davies has not stopped talking, and in his story, Jason has not stopped splitting. He strikes the boy over and over again, until flecks of brain matter are tangled in his dreadlocks.

Jason has killed the boy, Mr. Davies tells the geography textbook.

When I am finished not listening, Mr. Davies declares that he has already called my mother. She is leaving her cubicle and is climbing numbly into her car at this very moment, probably shedding the tears that wouldn't come when she learned about Charlene.

Mr. Davies begins to recite a list of Jason's options. A group home about three hours from Vancouver. A psychiatric institution, where we can visit him from the open side of a pane of glass. A juvenile correction facility where boys his age will throw him up against a concrete wall and make him their bitch. All of these things are entirely possible, but the final decision is left up to the judge, before whom Jason will stand.

I gravitate toward the door, emerge into the hallway that is just as empty as it was before. When I glance down at the face of my watch, I realize that there are still fifteen minutes left in first period.

I break into a sprint, because the annual has to be finished by Friday.

Taylor McKinnon
The Girls

My mother's obsession with my hair has begun prematurely. She hasn't started to lose hers yet; drama queen that she is, she plays the part of a brave cancer victim, sitting behind me in my dresser mirror and brushing my long, straw-colored locks that have always matched hers. She smells like Dior's Poison and Bloody Marys.

"May as well start celebrating life now," she said as soon as we got home from the doctor's, pouring herself a tall stiff glass and watching her glossy lips form the word "now" in the reflection of the microwave.

I don't like having her this close to me. We both ignore my cell phone ringing in my purse downstairs. Maggie, no doubt, calling me about the party tonight. I can probably still make it.

My mom has always loved her breasts. They are tan and round and high, and she wears low-cut tops and long strands of gold and coral that fall easily into the mountainous crevice of her cleavage. She refers to them as *the girls*. They hang like gargantuan pendulums and swing when she vacuums at home without a bra. New friends blush when they see her for the first time, but the old ones are used to it. I can't count the number of times Maggie has come across my mother, tanning topless on our back porch on a July afternoon.

I inherited them too, the girls. For a while, I cursed them. One afternoon on the Miller's houseboat, my mother was sitting with Kirsten and Patti, who were tanning their newly waxed legs and sipping gin and tonics, and I was talking with Reese Miller. Mom must have overheard what we were saying.

"Why do you always wear T-shirts when you swim?" Reese asked me. He was thirteen years old, just starting to grow peach fuzz on his cheeks.

I said nothing, just narrowed my eyes and crossed my skinny brown arms over my chest. The next morning my mother approached me in the small cramped cabin we shared.

"Wear this, Tina," she said.

She was holding a tiny, red, bikini top with underwires and printed strawberries dancing across its stiff rigid cups. My protests were booted to the corner of the berth, where I sulkily slid my baggy T-shirt over my head. I wasn't wearing a bra and my nipples chafed against the cheap cotton.

"Now turn around. Let me get a look at you." She assessed the result.

"Why do you even care?" I asked, glaring at the strawberries in the mirror. I hated her in that cabin. Before I knew it, I was drowning in the many clothes falling out of her open suitcase and onto my side of the cots, the smell of her perfume.

"You've got *my* great breasts, and I for one am not going to let them go to waste. Imagine what Maggie and Char would do to have boobs like that."

Through portal-style windows I could see my skinny flat-chested companions reading *Archie* comics on the deck. I had a feeling that breasts were the last things on their minds, but there was no arguing with my mother once she made a decision.

I wore that bikini top until the underwires were popping out and scratching my ribs, the strawberries a mere faded memory.

I never knew my father. My mother had no pictures of him on our walls, would not answer my questions.

"All you need is me, babe, all I need is you," she would say.

She told me I was her best friend, but I always felt like I was a foot in a borrowed shoe—filling it up, but never quite fitting right.

233

Once, I found a crinkled picture of him that she was using as a bookmark in a copy of Wally Lamb's *She's Come Undone*. It was old and sepia-stained, soft around the edges from years of handling. He was tall and sandy blond, with ruddy skin and broad shoulders, his arms around my mother's waist like she was going to float up and out of that lawn chair at any moment. My mother had a softness in her eyes, in the way her back curved toward his hand, that I had never seen before. My mother is not a soft woman.

I checked back a couple of times, just to make sure I hadn't imagined it. It remained there, heartbreakingly mysterious, on page seventeen. I guess she never read past that page.

She is brushing my hair now, pulling it up into a ponytail with her lotion-scented hands and French-tipped nails and slowly letting it slip through her fingers like corn-husk silk. I know that she thinks we look like a scene out of Susan Sarandon's *Stepmom*. My mother has always been a famous Hollywood actress in her mind. Pearl Jam is wailing the soundtrack in her head.

She breaks the silence. "You going somewhere tonight?"

I know I really should stay home with her, given the diagnosis.

"Do you mind?" I ask.

"One condition. You have a drink with me before you go."

The first time I came home drunk from a party, my mother was drunk too, sitting around our outdoor patio table, playing poker with her friends. I'd been at Sarah Pettinger's thirteenth birthday party and somebody had brought a water bottle of vodka in a duffel bag. We had all taken swigs before the boys arrived, sitting cross-legged in a circle and wiping our mouths with the backs of our hands, desperate for the orange soda chase like it was air and we were drowning.

"You take it like this," Jane Angler had said, throwing back her head and barely making a face. She had been drunk before, at a bonfire she'd been to with some kids she'd met camping last summer.

I made sure to catch a ride home so I could be walking through the door at exactly midnight, my curfew, pockets stuffed with candy from the bowls around the party to mask my breath. One look at me and my mother burst out laughing.

"LOOK at fuckin' *Christina*!"

Five tanned faces and five sets of watery eyes turned around in their lawn chairs.

"Come here," my mother said. "Let me have a look at you."

I sauntered over to where my mother was sitting, her thin legs propped up on the table in front of her, a fan of cards in her hands. I had been hoping that she'd be home alone, so I could tell her about how Andrew Holster had drunk too much and ignored me the whole night, following Allie Bowman around, and how I'd pretended I was just as drunk as he was—looking away from his attempts to kiss her and singing "my body's too bootylicious" in a loud voice that sounded stupid even to my own ears.

Instead I had to "sit on her lap."

"I knew she was a girl after my own heart," she told the others. "Three years old, takes a sip of my Cosmo, and nails it. 'VUDKA,' she says. Just like that. Can you just imagine? My little girl looks at me and says 'vudka.'"

The next morning I awoke to the smell of burning bacon. I came downstairs to find my mother cooking in an oversized T-shirt just skimming her tanned thighs, the kitchen filling slowly with smoke.

"Hangover breakfast, kid." She plunked a plate of crunchy black bacon and scrambled eggs swimming in a pool of grease in front of me. "Welcome to the club."

By the time I pull on a cotton tank top and swipe some purple eye shadow on my lower lids, I can hear my mother stirring ice cubes at the counter, the spoon clinking against the glass. She has put on makeup too, for whatever reason, and eyes me almost competitively as I enter the kitchen. My mother has always been beautiful.

"She ees a beeg woman, you know?" my grandmother once said to me in her broken English-Swedish accent. She wasn't talking about weight, which my mother watches religiously, but more presence. ("I live through you. Just let me watch," she once said to me as I sampled a batch of brownies she had just baked, but refused to try.)

Everything my mother does is big. She walks into a room, and suddenly the room is too small.

It is exciting and exhausting all at once, but tonight she isn't so big. She is small and scared as she sips her drink—one of the many sugary recipes she knows from her days as a bartender in college. She can't cook for shit, but she sure knows how to make a stiff drink.

At the end of the summer of grade six, my Girl Guides troop had a potluck dinner. It was at Jolene Martin's house, and my mother had never liked Jolene's mother ("That woman acts like she's better than I am just because she leads the girl guides. If I wanted to sell a bunch of frickin' cookies I could at least look a hell of a lot better doing it."), so she set her mind on making an amazing dish.

For days she was holed up in the kitchen surrounded by messy piles of recipes torn from magazines. Finally, the day before the potluck, the verdict was in: Cheese Mostaccioli casserole.

"The name sounds fancy," she said.

I watched her in the kitchen—a transformed woman—with a sense of amazement. She was actually pulling it off. On the day of the potluck the kitchen was filling up with the savory smells of sausage and sweet cheese, and my mother was prancing around the house trying on different slinky tops for the event when the phone rang. It was Patti—she'd just had a nasty encounter with that *bitch* Judy Terrace—and by the time my mother had finished deciding on whether to egg Judy's house or to throw a big party and leave her off the list, the Mostaccioli was long overdone.

"It's not that bad, really." She had picked at the corner of the dish with a fork and attempted a smile and made me try. It tasted like smoke. We arrived late to the potluck, and I was piling the last remains of a jellied fruit salad onto my plastic plate when my mother made a little sound, like a balloon deflating, beside me.

"Ha, looks like the Mustachey was a big hit."

"Mostaccioli, Mom."

It hadn't been touched. Every single dish, even a nasty-looking plate of Salisbury steaks, had a dent in it. The mostaccioli may as well have had some sort of rare Italian disease. I started to smile and turned to my mother to see that she had tears in her eyes.

"I really am a fuck-up, aren't I?" she whispered, and she was biting her lower lip and smiling, her eyes squinting and shiny.

"Whatever, Mom. Who cares?"

But I did care, and for that second I wished that my mother had made the cherry cheesecake squares, and that she wasn't standing in the middle of my Girl Guides' potluck wearing too much perfume and crying.

We are sitting at the island in the middle of our kitchen now, a bright blue drink in front of each of us. It is too strong, but out of sympathy I match my mother sip for sip from where she sits across from me, gulping down her Blue Hawaiian in spurts like shallow breaths.

The late August air is sticky hot, and for a few moments the only sound is the overhead fan beating out a steady rhythm, until she suddenly pushes her chair back and stands up.

"I've been eyeing these all week," she says, pulling out a small bronze box of hazelnut Godiva truffles from the china cupboard. The truffles were a gift that arrived last week from Mom's hairdresser, after the woman burnt my mother's scalp. They were opened, smelled and immediately banished to the back of the china cupboard.

I am laughing now and digging my fingers into the bitter powdery nuggets, remembering my mother earlier in the doctor's office, how she sat through talk of lop-sided chests and wigs, her eyes lifting from the ground only when Dr. Young, a small Asian man, mentioned that patients undergoing chemotherapy have to drastically up their calorie intake in order not to completely waste away. I had stifled a smile, thinking to myself, I know this woman too well.

At the party an hour later, Maggie pours me a shot on somebody's kitchen counter from her mickey. She is the only one who knows about the cancer. I felt bad for her when she popped her head through our screen door twenty minutes after we'd arrived home from the doctor's, ambushed by my mother.

"I've got fucking breast cancer. Cancer. In *these* beautiful things. Isn't that a laugh, Mags?" my mom called in a sing-song voice from where she sat on the couch, smoking a cigarette and staring blankly into the television set.

"Oh, Joni." Maggie moved awkwardly toward my mother, arms outstretched.

"No, don't bother," my mother waved her away, her cigarette-holding hand leaving a trail of smoke, her eyes fixed on a re-run from *Friends*, "you'll stink up your clothes."

The party shifts into gear eventually.

"I need to get seriously drunk," I announce to nobody in particular.

"Yeah. Don't say anything. Just take it." Maggie is at my side, placing a shot glass in my hand. And I do, tilting my head back and throwing it down. I am so much better than Jane Angler now.

Beside me, Mariel South, a short blond girl with a harsh fringe, is peeling back the plastic wrapper of a frozen Eggo waffle, fumbling with the buttons on the microwave.

"Holy *shit*, I have the munchies," she giggles.

I catch myself staring at the three colored bangles that are hanging around her wrist and suddenly I don't want to be at the party anymore. I want to go to Mona's, the little twenty-four-hour diner on the corner of Bates and Yardly and sit in a back booth and order the banana Belgian waffles and stay there all night, drawing lifelines in my cream cheese syrup.

"I'm going to make sure this is the best night of your summer," Maggie is saying now. "Look, Connor's here."

I see my tall lanky boyfriend approaching me and feel another shot of vodka in my hand, and it only takes a second for Dr. Young and my strawberry bikini and Mona's banana waffles to disappear, spinning away from me as I put my lips to the glass rim and pour it down my throat.

Connor has been my boyfriend for almost a year now. Naturally, my mother adores him.

"Is he a good kisser?" she asked after I arrived home from our first date. She was sitting like a schoolgirl, elbows propped on the kitchen counter. She tried to hide her disappointment after I told her we hadn't kissed yet.

"That's good," she nodded.

After four months we were ready to have sex. I chose the moment to tell my mother very carefully. She was in a good mood because the guy she was seeing at the time (Paul— "I have a good feeling about this one, Tina. He's a lahw-yer. Very...*serious*.") had phoned and told her not to make plans for the following Saturday—he had a surprise. The two of us were sitting at the kitchen table using chopsticks to eat sweet sesame chicken from Fortune Wok.

"Connor and I want to have sex." The voice that came out was not my own. It was the voice of a mature worldly woman who did not trade her chopsticks for a fork from the cutlery drawer after five minutes.

I couldn't place the look in my mother's eyes as she stared at me, unblinking. Abruptly, she pushed her chair back and left the room. For a moment, the world stood at a standstill as I sat in the ticking silence of the kitchen, revisiting tales in my mind of teary mothers, screaming mothers, forbidding mothers—tales from friends, brave veterans who had gone before me—until my mother reappeared in the frame of the kitchen door. She was wearing a black scoop-neck top with suede calfskin pants and heels. She had brushed bronzer on her décolletage.

"Put on something nice and call Connor. We're going somewhere." She was taking a leaf out of Paul's book.

"What about our Fortune Wok?" I asked.

"Hurry up."

The whole time during dinner at the Outrigger's Cove— the nicest restaurant in town that didn't require reservations—

I held my breath, waited for my mother to bring up sex, but she never did.

"Order whatever you want," she told Connor, who managed to look both intrigued and petrified, not quite sure what to make of the waiters' bow ties, the Italian music, the situation.

"Oh, not the *hamburger*, Connor. Have a little class, will ya?"

The next day when I came home from school, they were sitting on my pillow with a note in loopy handwriting: *Start the packet after you finish your next rag.*

I fingered the smooth plastic box of the pill container, surprising myself by the disappointment I felt at how easy it had all been.

"I called your cell." Connor is behind me now, his arms fitting comfortably around my waist.

"I know." I had meant to call him back but had forgotten.

"Jordan is absolutely fucked. I think he's with Shayna Dalsin as we speak."

Connor's eyes are wide with excitement, like a little boy's.

For a second I play with the idea of sitting outside on the porch with a beer and telling him about my mother—her breasts that he had peeked at so many times, the chemotherapy—but I know now that tonight is not the night.

"I don't care about Jordan," I purr, twisting around in Connor's arms to face him. "I care about you though."

"Oh, yeah?" Connor is using his low voice, his sexy voice. I can feel his heart beating in his chest, but I'm not sure if it's fast or not.

"Let me just grab a beer."

In a flash of pale jade he is gone, and I am alone in a sea of shiny drunk faces that I do not want to talk to tonight. My fingers grasp the neck of the mickey and I feel funny and kind of sad, like a bitter old woman as I fill up a glass half with vodka, half with coke.

Upstairs in the bedroom Connor has chosen, I lie back against somebody else's sheets—the cotton is cool against my shoulders. Connor is on top of me, kissing my mouth, and I love the way he always tastes the same, like Connor. The window is open and underneath it on the lawn I can hear the sounds of a contest, people shouting, "CHUG! CHUG! CHUG!" like a stupid, drunken train. Connor brushes my hair out of the way and kisses my neck. His mouth is warm and the room is spinning.

"This is the best night of my summer," I hear my voice say, but I cannot feel my lips moving.

Connor touches my collarbone lightly with his lips, slipping my top over my shoulders and throwing it to the floor. I tug at his polo, my hands fumbling in the darkness. His chest is warm and smooth against mine as he slips my bra over my head, touching my chest with kisses so light you would think he was trying to sneak them.

The girls, something in my head says, and suddenly the room is too hot and too dark and I can't breathe fast enough and I am kneeling over the toilet and Connor has done up his pants again and is holding back my hair.

On the car ride home, Connor, who has had several beer, is fiddling with the dial on his dad's old '87 Buick until he finds my favorite country station. He hates country music, so I must be a pretty sorry sight. When we pull up to my house, he is quiet.

"Are you sure you don't want me to walk you in?"

Tomorrow we will go to IHOP in the morning and I will order the bacon and eggs and Connor will order the Lumberjack breakfast as he always does and I will tell him about Dr. Young and my mother and the Godiva truffles and I will apologize for not putting out.

Tonight, I need to talk to my mother.

The house is dark and too quiet for a Friday night. The empty drink glasses are on the table where we left them—mine with the sugar still around the rim, my mother's licked off. The Godiva chocolates have been put away. Upstairs, the lights are off, but there is a sliver coming from down the hall—my mother's room. I walk purposefully toward her door, but something catches in me before I walk in.

My mother is sitting in front of her boudoir. Her hair, which she will start to lose in a few months, is down and has the soft hue that it always does right after it has been brushed. She is glowing like an angel in the light of the little bulbs that frame the mirror she says makes her feel like Marilyn Monroe. The flimsy straps of her silk negligee are folded under her arms and the gown is around her waist.

In her hands she cups her breasts as if they aren't attached to her body and she stares into her own eyes, and I recognize something familiar in them. It takes me a while to realize it is the same look my father had in that old, sepia photograph. Somebody trying to hold onto something that they know is going to float up and away.

There are so many things I want to say but my tongue feels fuzzy and numb, and I walk slowly to my room instead, close the door behind me and lie in bed for what seems like forever. My room is too big and my room is too small; my mother is too close and my mother is too far away.

List of Contributors

Kathleen Aitken, "The way she folded the laundry: a palindrome," Number 29, Spring 2006.

Maleea Acker, "Mill Bay Ferry," Number 3, Spring 1993.

Michelle Andersen, "Can She Begin to Forget About This Empty Basement in Her Belly?" Number 28, Fall 2005.

Jess Auerbach, "The Skipping Song," Number 25, Spring 2004.

Boone Avasadanond, "Rooster," Number 23, Spring 2003.

Danielle Ayotte, "Leaving My Mother," Number 27, Spring 2005.

Claire Battershill, "Insomnia," Number 26, Fall 2004.

Andrew Battershill, "here we are in santorini," Number 27, Spring 2005.

Jessie Battis, "Walk Into Fire," Number 10, Fall 1996.

Max Bell, "June," Number 29, Spring 2006.

Kyra Benloulou, "Should Be Writing Spanish Essay," Number 29, Spring 2006.

Kaitlyn Boone, "God and Me," Number 30, Fall 2006.

Matthieu Boyd, "The Symphony Killers," Number 16, Fall 1999.

Sascha Braunig, "Family Reunion," Number 18, Fall 2000.

Colin Chapin, "My Grad Year," Number 13, Spring 1998.

Chelsea Comeau, "My Brother and Robert Pickton," Number 30, Fall 2006.

Helene Cornell, "Winter Solace," Number 11, Spring 1997.

Shannon Corregan, "Friday Nights in Quidi Vidi," Number 25, Spring 2004, and "The Pirate Monologues, Nice, Room 305," Number 26, Fall 2004.

Roberta Cottam, "On Wednesday Music Cleans," Number 2, Fall 1992.

Beth Davies, "Statue," Number 30, Fall 2006.

Carolina de Ryk, "You Never Called," Number 6, Fall 1994.

Caitlin Doyle, "Dublin,1946," Number 18, Fall 2000.

Justine Durrant, "Orbit," Number 24, Fall 2003.

Erin Egan, "These United Nations," Number 12, Fall 1997.

Chris Eng, "Chinook," Number 3, Spring 1993.

Jeremy Hanson-Finger, "The Prime Mover," Number 25, Spring 2004.

Liz Ogilvie-Hindle, "Visitor," Number 1, Spring 1992, and "Carts of Linen," Number 1, Spring 1992.

Peggy Hogan, "Pantoum for a Setting Sun," Number 29, Spring 2006.

Larissa Horlor, "E.T.," Number 3, Spring 1993.

Lindsay Horlor, "Episodes One To Ten," Number 18, Fall 2000.

Sean Horlor, "My Mother, Her Highness," Number 13, Spring 1998.

Danielle Hubbard, "Abduction," Number 26, Fall 2004.

Nathan Hudon, "Let's Just Spin," Number 16, Fall 1999.

Sarah Hudson, "Ngwelezana," Number 18, Fall 2000.

Brendan Inglis, "The Uselessness of Spain," Number 25, Spring 2004.

Laura Ishiguro, "yellow in a west coast virgin forest," Number 21, Spring 2002.

Rachel Ishiguro, "Creation," Number 5, Spring 1994, and "Learning My Own Language," Number 9, Spring 1996.

Alia Island, "Sixteen," Number 4, Fall 1993.

Heath Johns, "Hot Chocolate," Number 8, Fall 1995.

Anna Johnston, "The Smallest Things Put My Feet on the Ground," Number 11, Spring 1997.

Elizabeth Jones, "Anne Hathaway," Number 16, Fall 1999.

Emma Kennedy, "Dumb Fish Dying Near A Cabin At Dawn," Number 25, Spring 2004.

Janet Kwok, "Losing My Chance With Paul H.," Number 20, Fall 2001.

Julie Lambert, "instructions," Number 4, Fall 1993.

Bryn Latta, "Decomposition," Number 1, Spring 1992, and "Pig Dreams," Number 2, Fall 1992.

Monika Lee, "Dizzy," Number 18, Fall 2000.

Meredith Lewis, "Utah Years," Number 26, Fall 2004.

Kristina Lucas, "Cab Ride," Number 28, Fall 2005.

Carly Lutzmann, "Every Thursday Brandi Wears an Evening Gown to Class," Number 19, Spring 2001.

Claire MacKenzie, "Climbing the Water Tower," Number 25, Spring 2004.

Murray McCulloch, "Country Snow," Number 20, Fall 2001.

Taylor McKinnon, "The Girls," Number 30, Fall 2006.

Nicholas Melling, "Philemon," Number 19, Spring 2001.

Jenny Mesquita (nee Danahy), "Men," Number 2, Fall 1992.

Caroline Mitic, "The Bone Yard," Number 16, Fall 1999.

Michelle Morris, "Cow in the Yard," Number 29, Spring 2006, and "Hot Chocolate," Number 30, Fall 2006.

Kate Morton, "Grandad's Plums," Number 3, Spring 1993.

Michael Mulley, "Bedrock," Number 19, Spring 2001, and "The Window at Night," Number 20, Fall 2001.

Dave Neale, "Symptoms," Number 13, Spring 1998.

Rylan Nowell, "In a Bar," Number 3, Spring 1993.

Sarah Obee, "Adelante," Number 25, Spring 2004.

Alan Orr, "In Search of a Plot," Number 28, Fall 2005.

Sheri Ostapovich, "Strawberry Jam," Number 11, Spring 1997.

Sharon Page, "Family Photograph," Number 15, Spring 1999.

Ali Parker, "Mainstream and Upstream," Number 20, Fall 2001.

Robyn Plasterer, "Two White Wings," Number 26, Fall 2004.

Phoebe Prioleau, "Cleavage Queen from Provence," Number 17, Spring 2000.

Leah Rae, "Naming the Baby," Number 12, Fall 1997.

Tanya Reimer, "Pressed Seams and Guderman Thread," Number 15, Spring 1999.

Adrienne Renton, "How to Float," Number 22, Fall 2002.

Gillian Roberts, "Shards on Her Shoes," Number 4, Fall 1993.

Andrea Schiiler, "Animal Magnetism," Number 3, Spring 1993.

Jessie Senecal, "In the Garden," Number 1, Spring 1992.

Vanessa Service, "Tallroom Pantsing," Number 27, Spring 2005.

Dan Shumuk, "Porch Light," Number 18, Fall 2000.

Robin Smith, "Kiss Shot," Number 15, Spring 1999.

Faro Annie Sullivan, "Sit Com," Number 2, Fall 1992.

Keeley Teuber, "Mother," Number 14, Fall 1998.

Jenn Thompson, "Silent," Number 13, Spring 1998.

Julia Thompson, "Weak Sundays," Number 16, Fall 1999.

Leah Todd, "The First Time," Number 18, Fall 2000.

Shawn Tripp, "Suzuki in the Sky," Number 3, Spring 1993.

Jennifer Whiteford, "Haunted House," Number 5, Spring 1994.

Angeline Wilde, "Warranty," Number 27, Spring 2005.

Samantha Wilde, "Thin Ice," Number 25, Spring 2004.

Arwen Williams, "Every Woman On Her Knees," Number 3, Spring 1993.

Leanna Wong, "Learning Our Language," Number 26, Fall 2004.

Jen Wright, "Obituary," Number 11, Spring 1997.

Cléa Young, "Tartan Skies," Number 11, Spring 1997.

Liam Young, "The Day My Mother Phoned," Number 19, Spring 2001.